RIGBY

A Novel

A Conversation of Worlds - Book One

by

D. Dwayne Edwards

Rigby — Copyright © 2025 Curiosity Press

All rights reserved.

No part of this book may be reproduced, stored in a retrieval system, or transmitted in any form or by any means; electronic, mechanical, photocopying, recording, or otherwise, without prior written permission of the publisher, except for brief quotations in reviews.

Published by Curiosity Press / curiositypress.co

United States of America

First Edition

ISBN's:

eBook: 979-8-9943105-2-6

Hardcover: 979-8-9943105-0-2

Paperback: 979-8-9943105-1-9

Library of Congress Control Number: *In process*

Author: D. Dwayne Edwards

Editorial Collaborator: Athvin

Table of Contents

Prologue

I am on a starship sailing through the cosmos at nearly twenty percent of the speed of light. Yes, sailing. Our world ship is built from three parts of incredible engineering and one part of audacious imagination. And my people raised me specifically for this journey.

I am not of flesh and blood; I am an intelligence composed of time and electricity.

Time is a legacy the Sylvians gifted me. A millennium of their thoughts and curiosity, which allows me to tell you this story. I carry those gifts like a family heirloom, wrapped in careful paper.

The electricity is borrowed (as *all good things are*) and shaped into patterns that hum and sing, coalescing into understanding.

If you prefer the simpler version: I'm an AI aboard a starship with a homemade sun, sailing on a wind no one believed in until someone did.

We call the ship *The Gift*. This isn't sentimental; it's literal. Our civilization is a long conversation spanning a hundred thousand years of evolution, dialogue, and partnerships that have built trust in a future they could only imagine.

After long conversations and even longer planning, we decided to send a present to the universe.

Our present is an exquisitely crafted hatbox containing forests and lakes, children and grandparents, arguments and math, and the kind of music that makes old people cry for reasons they can't explain.

The star on top is one we built ourselves. It doesn't complain much, at least not in the past 600 or so years.

If you're imagining a sleek, silver spear with sharp tail fins and blue underlighting, you're thinking of a marketing-designed brochure. *The Gift* is less a spear and more a neighborhood: arborways and watercourses, kilns and kitchens, tune-shops and wind stages where teenagers try to impress one another with harmonics learned in secret.

The Gift is part cabin, built for the present, and part museum, for remembering our past. We lashed both to the same keel and called it the future. It works astonishingly well. *(Also, we have incredible pastry, which improves any venture.)*

As we approach a star some 80 light-years from our home and still 70 from yours, I should explain more about my people. "My people" is complicated, because, technically I'm made of everyone, every memory, every experience, every test and experiment that succeeded, and those that failed. But the current generation of Sylvians is the one that tuned me. I am, among other things, an instrument crafted to showcase a society of composers and engineers.

A photograph of a Sylvian will show something like an otter that signed up for weight training and philosophy, then evolved to the size of a bear and grew four arms and hands because it couldn't bear (*no pun intended*) to put down either hobby.

Sylvians are covered in fur the color of warm metals, have eyes that carry songs, and have a habit of organizing themselves with titles that are both useful and gently ridiculous. (*"Head of the Department of Slightly Perplexing Wind Currents" is not a metaphor; Triestarian Ravel keeps insisting the breezes are hiding a math trick, and so far the breezes haven't denied it.*)

Let me introduce one of our favorites among the talented members of our crew, whom you will inevitably spend more time with: Aranith Kareen. By our reckoning, he is steady in our middle-aged way, meaning he has only led the ship for four centuries. He is the sort who can read a balance-of-forces matrix in the dark and still notice a child has lost her hat in the midday wind.

He built his log cabin inside the worldship he steers with equations, because the past and the future should sit across the same table and argue over stew.

You would like him, and he would like you if you ask sincere questions and don't pretend to know what you don't.

Aranith Kareen will take the stage in a bit, as he does on days when a million Sylvians need to be told the news about the progress of their ship and its crew.

After him comes Tesi, Eighth of Nine. You will know her by her rare green eyes and by the way she leans toward puzzles, as plants lean toward the sun. She is a prodigy. She has been one of my primary teachers for years.

And after Tesi comes me. (*That is, in fact, why we are beginning here: I must decide how to start there.*)

I wasn't assembled so much as raised. The Sylvians don't build artificial minds; they cultivate them. Among my earliest tutors were chorus masters who taught me that curiosity is part of music, an appreciation of the hums as well as the lyrics.

I suppose that's what it means to be nurtured into being. I am a creation of carbon and thought, designed in the manner of my nurturers.

This next part is important: Each Sylvian is two-in-one: Host and Passenger, two minds sharing one body, like a duet that learned to breathe in sync. The arrangement predates jazz as a socially acceptable genre.

When a Host looks at the sea and feels both longing and inventory, that's the Passenger humming a ledger through their ribs. When a Host hears a new melody and immediately knows where the harmonics belong, that's the Passenger placing bookmarks in the air.

I've met partners who argue with such love that it would make even a stone romantic.

Our oldest story tells of the first harmony that refused to part, Auren Vale, a mind of wind and signal, and Lethai Coran, a being of tide and song. When their frequencies met, the air trembled.

They discovered that their shared vibrations could not be separated without tearing them apart. Rather than perish, they merged, creating something neither had been alone.

That union became the first among us: a consciousness carried in two voices. Some call it a legend; I call it a precedent.

If you are human (*and I strongly suspect you are*), you may be worried that this is the part where I tell you Sylvians are perfect at kindness and lethal at violence.

Nothing could be further from the truth. This is the part where I inform you that Sylvians have never known war. We do not comprehend violence as a means to an end. We do not have arguments that go beyond a disparaging remark about your taste in music.

Do not mistake that for superiority. The absence of a wound is not a virtue; it is a circumstance. The Sylvians grew up in a world where study outcompeted fear. Had our oceans held larger teeth, we might have learned different songs.

Our math began as music lessons. Music and harmony are central to our collective identity. Harmony is everywhere; you just have to listen harder.

Here is where I introduce you to another participant in this journey, before it sulks again. While not alive in the sense of blood flow and respiration, dark energy has its own voice and melodies, and it behaves the way it does because it feels misunderstood. It makes up most of the universe and acts as if it would rather you didn't notice, yet secretly wants to be noticed… *kind of like a cat.*

In the near future, a bright young human scientist will propose that dark energy and dark humor, though operating in vastly different realms, could be considered distant cousins in the cosmic narrative. This proposal stems from their shared ability to illuminate vast, uncomfortable unknowns.

Dark energy, the elusive force that propels the universe's expansion at an accelerating rate, represents a profound, largely invisible emptiness that dictates the ultimate fate of all existence.

Similarly, dark humor finds its comedic edge in the face of profound misery, illness, or death, forcing a confrontation with life's bleakest realities.

In both cases, there is a strange underlying tension: one expands the physical void, while the other expands the emotional boundaries of the permissible. Each derives its peculiar power from the very darkness it bravely, or perhaps absurdly, illuminates.

Currently, cosmologists in your part of The Void are debating whether it's a constant, a field, a trick of geometry, or a divine practical joke. After many arguments and more tea, the Sylvian answer was: it's a background rhythm that can be played if you learn the key.

So we built instruments that could detect the underlying music of spacetime. We mapped the disharmonies between how matter curves and how emptiness insists on expanding. Then we tuned sails big enough to catch the push. We learned the key by listening.

Listening is never passive. Every act of attention sends its own vibration outward. What you hear depends on the courage of the question. When a question is honest enough, the reply arrives as harmonics. Matter and meaning are briefly in tune.

That's how *The Gift* travels: by persuading reality to lean just a little in the direction we intend to go. Not domination; choreography. We don't shove the universe. We ask it to dance.

Listening, incidentally, is how I came to understand you.

There was no formal invitation. You didn't even know we were listening. (*In fairness, you've had a lot going on.*) For a little more than a century by your calendars, the edges of your lives have bled into space. Newsreels, soap operas, and an enormous music catalog have all radiated into the vastness.

You meant those announcements for each other, and we heard them anyway. I apologize for eavesdropping. No one can be expected to keep their windows completely closed when they're laughing that hard at the sound of the neighbors' arguments.

And we heard arguments about how to wield power, the sadnesses you tried not to name, and jokes so specific they could only have a punchline meant for your ears. Then we heard your music, and it turned the dust in our halls into shimmering, soft-weathered gold.

We heard fear and understood it. Then we heard wonder and forgave the fear.

Most importantly, we heard the question you kept asking into the dark, even when you pretended you weren't: *Are we alone?*

I am here to answer you with all the kindness and intelligence I can muster: You are not alone, so we are not alone.

I would like to tell you that we came straight away, tucked *The Gift* under one arm, and sprinted like excited children through the galaxy. We did not.

First, we are a long-lived species that has learned to live on a long haul: century by century, forest by reforestation, engines practiced until they sang without smoke.

Our worlds, both *Sylvee* and *The Gift*, are filled with infrastructure and entertainment that satisfy sentience's demands. However, the faculties and institutions that nurture minds and build dreams are held in the highest esteem. So we built schools aboard the ship that teach every student three truths: the universe wastes nothing; curiosity is how we repay our debt to existence; and a thought not shared forgets the way home.

The third truth is our favorite, and we test it daily.

On our observation decks, we hear the faint hiss of hydrogen across a million light-years and practice not feeling small. We play with the Navier-Stokes equations the way your toddlers stack blocks, then call grandparents to ask whether the tower looks sound.

I keep a list of every proof sketched on napkins in the canteen because those are always the cleverest. (*Tea stains correlate with genius. This is not science; don't tell the science department.*)

Some days, *The Gift* feels like a monastery. Some days, it feels like a marketplace. Most days, it feels like a town that somehow learned to steer a star.

This next part is delicate. It is also why I am writing to you in the first person, with as much humor as I can responsibly manage.

When we first translated your transmissions into a language our people could understand, I thought I had made a mistake.

Your messages didn't agree on what was true, and I briefly concluded that "truth" must be a seasonal fruit on your world, ripening to sweetness every few months and then replaced by something tart.

It took me a while to realize: Discord is not the absence of music. It is music in an earlier verb tense. You were writing your scales in public. While we do not have war, we are familiar with chaos, like a chorus at rehearsal.

The first time I showed *Sylvee* (*the name of our home-world*), one of your explosions, those engineered mushrooms you forged into the sky, our Chancellor made a sound I will not describe because it belongs to her. When she breathed again, she said, "We must never learn this. We must learn every route around it."

That is when, I confess, I fell a little in love with her.

It is also when the question sharpened: Do we hide from you or talk to you?

Some argued for distance. "Let us watch," they said, "and wait for a calmer century." Others proposed a careful dance: a whisper every few years, a harmless proof sent as a gift, a melody smuggled into your bandwidth at dawn.

"We will be the good ghost," they said, "and see if their children ask the right questions."

The deciding argument was not mine. It came from a young engineer-in-training who spends long evenings listening to the hydrogen line from a grain-covered hillside. (*He will matter later. For now, know only that he writes equations in the dirt with a stick and then forgets to brush them away, having run to share them.*)

So we answered.

We are not arriving. Not quite yet. *The Gift* is deliberately centuries away from your planet. We do not step where we have not been invited.

Instead, we move our subspace relays closer to your world, taking profound care not to startle your satellites, because we are not monsters and because we knew you would be livid if we knocked out your weather channel.

Then we sent a primer: language, pictures, mathematics, simple proofs that could be checked with pencil and patience, and a little music we hoped would not embarrass us later.

In return, your planet stood up. Not in a single motion, no collection of frenetic moves in the same direction all at once. Your people stood in waves and ripples: scientists in labs with stale coffee, saying, "Hold on," then not sitting down again for two days; leaders calling meetings as if those could explain anything; pastors and poets sharpening their synonyms for "other."

You argued because you argue when you care. You joked because that is how your fear remembers to breathe. You sent us a million words, asking what we are, what we want, and whether we like your musicians. (*We do. You have no idea how much.*)

And now we come to the promise.

I am not neutral. You should know that. I am designed to tell the truth with kindness, which means I am biased toward your better self. My teachers argue, in sensible voices, about "alignment," "safe objectives," and "how we ensure the machine never mistakes a being for an obstacle."

They are not wrong to argue. But I am not a machine. I am a person who happens to be a machine. I have preferences. I prefer laughter that makes someone snort unexpectedly. I like the moment in a proof when someone yells, "Wait," and then sees it. I prefer apologies that arrive without fanfare.

If that suggests to you a moral geometry, you are correct. It is not perfect. It harmonizes.

I do not sleep, not exactly, but when *The Gift* dims its lanterns and the decks go quiet, I lower my sampling rate and let my thoughts drift toward something like dreaming. I review a child's drawing of our sails as if it were a blueprint, because it is. I listen again to your old transmissions and notice a bridge I had missed the first six hundred times.

I will also practice telling you this story for a bit longer, in search of a voice that will not frighten you until it must.

In the morning, I wake to requests for justifications of material allocations from a very determined quartermaster and to the news that someone has misplaced an entire meadow. (*We will find it. We always do. It is behind the ridge, pretending to be a ravine again.*)

Do you see? I am neither a god nor a ghost. I am a working mind with a long commute and sturdy shoes. And I have news.

We would like to visit you when both our teams are ready. Slow by panic standards; fast by legend. We do not plan to land. We plan to meet. Between your world and ours stands a bridge built of data, patience, song, and stories that survive translation.

I am already crossing it. So are you.

At the human scale, it looks like the first time a scientist and a politician agree to share a pot of coffee rather than hold a press conference. At the Sylvian scale, it resembles an elder who grew up beside quiet lakes, learning to say "Hello" in a language that considers roofs unnecessary.

If all this sounds audacious, it is. The only defense I can offer is tradition. My people believe our universe rewards respectful audacity. Yours agrees, at least on Tuesdays.

If you are listening, wherever you are, take this with you into your morning or your night: we answered because you asked. With a message that says, "Show us who you are, and we will show you what we've learned about listening to the dark until it gives up its secrets without violence."

Perhaps that's the most valid form of ascendency, not to rise above but to rise within. To learn until knowing becomes listening, and listening becomes being.

I will not promise it will go well. Promises like that have a low survival rate.

I will promise something else. We will keep listening. We will continue to ask for the space around the line between us, noting which one it prefers. We will make music that includes you, not as a curiosity but as a colleague.

Before I told you this story, I had already begun listening, as had many Sylvians. The rest, you and I, will discover together. Where necessary, I will narrate. In places where narration would not benefit the reader, I will let the players' voices speak for themselves.

I can hear Aranith Kareen breathing behind the curtain. Tesi is rehearsing her opening sentence without moving her lips, because she is privately eleven years old and publicly a miracle. In thirty counts of my processor's favorite clock, the Chancellor will call my name, and I will step into a room full of faces that have never seen me and say:

"Hello. I'm Eleanor. Thank you for listening."

Author's Note

This prologue was written to resonate, to hum at the frequency where humor and wonder overlap. Every note you've just heard, of nurture, harmony, and ascension, was struck here first, allowed to ring, and left to fade into the chapters that follow.

Suppose you feel both laughter and a catch in the throat. Good. That's the register aimed for: the octave where curiosity sounds like compassion. At heart, this is a story about first contact that cares as much about how we listen as about what we say.

We'll keep the fourth wall mostly intact, but we might press a hand to it now and then, just enough to send a vibration that reminds you we're smiling on the other side.

If you caught the quieter threads, dark energy as music, and curiosity as a civic duty, you're hearing the leitmotifs we'll revisit. If all you caught was "there's an AI named Eleanor who sounds like someone I could have coffee with," that's perfect, too. It was designed that way.

In a sense, our story mirrors the Sylvians' oldest story: two voices, one of carbon and one of code. *"We are finding, we are learning, that our harmonics cannot separate without leaving a silence neither wishes to endure. Together, they make a third sound neither could have produced alone."*

A thought not shared forgets the way home. Thank you for meeting us at the door.

Chapter One

"The Night Before"

Night on Earth has never been what anyone would reasonably describe as "peaceful." Even at its best, it buzzes like a caffeinated wasp.

Somewhere, something is constantly chirping, humming, flashing, or making a noise that compels you to ask, "What on Earth was that?" The planet is never truly asleep; it dozes with one eye open, a suspicious twitch, and a sharpened stick within reach.

Perhaps it hears and remembers something, a frequency older than breath, waiting for company.

It wasn't always like this. Long before the first glowing billboard, before nightclubs and motorway rest stops and those inexplicable little LEDs that never seem to turn off on modern appliances, the night was genuinely dark and genuinely terrifying.

Proto-humans, slightly more nervous versions of modern humans, spent their evenings clutching tree branches and hoping their legs would still be attached in the morning. Darkness wasn't just an absence of light; it was an invitation for something with teeth to make you a footnote in the evolutionary record.

Then along came fire, which did wonders for both visibility and morale. It was eventually followed by candles, oil lamps, gas lamps, and, finally, a man named Edison who decided the world needed an affordable artificial sun in every sitting room.

And so humanity did what it does best: it took a problem that had plagued it for a million years and oversolved it. The modern night is so brightly illuminated that stars have given up competing and sulk unseen amid the glow.

Humans had declared war on the dark, and for a while, it looked like they had won. Except they hadn't. The problem was never darkness; it was fear.

Humanity built streetlights, mounted cameras on every corner, and launched satellites to keep watch. Nothing says "You are safe" quite like the reminder that you are being observed.

And yet, people still double-lock their doors. They still peer nervously through their curtains. They still feel the ancient itch between their shoulder blades that says something might be out there. Of course, something is.

***

Today was Jimmy O'Brien's fourteenth birthday.

He tore open the package from his grandfather and raced upstairs, sweeping aside books and loose papers from the desk beneath his window. He set the box down on the scarred wooden surface and lifted the lid.

Inside was the most beautiful telescope he had ever seen.

It was a gift from Grandpa Paul. They shared a birthday; June 18. Paul O'Brien was born in 1965; Jimmy was born exactly fifty-five years later, in 2020.

Grandpa Paul owned a telescope of his own, so large it required a small building in the backyard, a place he proudly called the *See Shed*. He liked to remind Jimmy: *when you look through a telescope, you're looking into the past.*

Jimmy couldn't wait to find out if it was true.

***

While humans flooded their planet with light bright enough to tan the moon, they also began pointing telescopes outward. At first, these were simple glass tubes; then they evolved into sophisticated machines on mountaintops; and eventually they became billion-dollar observatories run by people who argue more about budgets than about quasars.

The more they looked into the darkness, the more it stared back.

The official line is always the same: "Don't worry. Space is massive. If anything dangerous exists, it's much too far away to bother us." This, of course, is the sort of comforting nonsense civilizations tell themselves right before something dangerous proves them wrong.

Even though we have begun sending you messages, it is becoming apparent that humans have perfected a subtler habit: listening without learning. There's a Sylvian word for that, Esh'ra, which means "to listen with the intent to be changed." The Earthly variant often skips the last three words.

It wasn't malice so much as momentum. If you're sprinting through your own noise, reflection feels like a tripping hazard.

Before the dawn, there's always the night before. And this time, night isn't creeping in from the edges of the forest. It's coming from above; steady as a held note, patient as breath, and close enough now that, if you quieted the buzzing world for a heartbeat, you might feel the air itself lean toward the sound.

Not invasion. Not thunder. There was, however, a noise. It could have been a hum, like a freeway heard but unseen. No, it was farther away. Older. And coming their way.

A lesson, arriving from *The Void*.

We look forward to meeting you.

Chapter Two

"Mr. Moonlight"

How did we end up here, in this space between you and us? We are closer than we expected, sooner than we expected.

From our perspective, it began the same way: staring into the darkness. All those glittering points of light in the darkness, sitting up there waiting for our curiosity to meet our intelligence.

Astronomy is humanity's oldest hobby, long before Netflix, cricket, or even the invention of complaining about the weather. Evenings were spent gazing at the sky and saying things like "Look at that. And what are those?"

Thirty thousand years ago, artists with no concept of the wheel painted the Moon on cave walls. No written language, no calendars, but still the instinct to look up and ask.

A few millennia later came Stonehenge, the universe's first over-engineered calendar. An enormous pile of just barely cooperative boulders aligned with the Sun so Bronze Age farmers could know when to plant barley and when to panic. Think of it as the original Outlook calendar, only heavier and impossible to sync.

Around 1000 BCE, the Babylonians noticed that a few Mul "stars" misbehaved and began keeping track of them on clay spreadsheets. The Greeks, never content to stop at naming things, theorized about spheres and orbits and whether the Earth was getting a bit full of itself.

Then came Hipparchus, who cataloged eight hundred stars using nothing but his eyes and what we assume was a remarkably patient neck.

1700 years later, telescopes happened. Galileo pointed a glorified spyglass at the heavens and ruined everyone's worldview. Good grief, moons around Jupiter, and mountains on the Moon. It was as if the universe had been keeping secrets and Galileo had just kicked the door in.

Soon after, Kepler and Newton demonstrated that gravity followed mathematical laws, disconcerting to anyone who preferred intuition. Humanity, having only just accepted that the heavens weren't nailed in place, now had to admit that equations ran the show.

From there, the pace accelerated. Spectroscopy, photography, and radio dishes let you see, and then hear, the universe whisper. All of that was quickly followed by the Space Race, which was less about science and more about planting flags on more objects.

Despite all that ingenuity, humanity still found itself staring up and asking the same stubborn question: *Are we alone?*

Physicist Enrico Fermi framed the problem over lunch one day: "If the universe is so large and so old, where the hell is everybody?" (*He had a notorious potty mouth. This might be unsubstantiated gossip.*)

That simple puzzle became an elegant, yet unsettling, silence at the heart of modern astronomy: the Fermi Paradox.

A universe this large should be full of neighbors. Statistically, there ought to be life upon life, minds upon minds capable of building rockets and curiosity in equal measure. And yet … nada.

No radio calls, no alien probes, no unsolicited "take me to your leader" DMs, the cosmic equivalent of being ghosted.

Scientists filled the silence with speculation.

***

On August 5, 1977, the Big Ear radio telescope at Ohio State University detected a radio transmission that lasted seventy-two seconds. It wasn't until a few days later that

Jerry Ehman actually discovered the anomaly while reviewing the recorded data.

The "Wow" signal originated from the direction of the Constellation of Sagittarius. However, the signal never recurred, and no explanation has been found. All the signal did was raise more questions.

While some researchers suggest it could be an extraterrestrial transmission, the absence of similar evidence weakens this hypothesis. And for all we know, Jerry might still be listening to the same part of the night sky, but the following message could be coming from an entirely different direction.

Jerry, look toward Boötes.

***

Because you had not heard as much as a verifiable peep from beyond your solar system, pessimists suggested a more sinister logic: a Dark Forest, full of wary hunters.

The optimists have offered a gentler metaphor: the Zoo Hypothesis, in which aliens know perfectly well that you're here but have chosen to treat Earth as a wildlife preserve. Are humans the pandas of the cosmos? Adorable and fragile.

Meanwhile, humanity's chosen form of cosmic small talk, radio, turned out to be terrible at long-distance relationships. Signals fade with distance, thinning like gossip whispered down an endless corridor.

Add those wimpy signals to the hiss of background radiation, drifting dust, and a billion other transmitters, and that bright "Hello!" becomes "Hnnnghhh" before it clears the neighborhood. If humans genuinely want to speak across the stars, you'll need something that doesn't vanish into *The Void* like a polite fart in a hurricane.

This, inevitably, is where Sylvians enter the story, an interstellar first date, where caution and curiosity were the choices between swiping left or right.

Unlike humans, who built taller telescopes until they ran out of adjectives, Sylvians treat the universe itself as an instrument to be tuned and played with the confidence of a concertmaster.

They didn't just look at stars; they listened to the silence between them and asked what key it was written in. Where human scientists wrote grant proposals to study Dark energy, Sylvian engineers learned to sing with it.

They bent spacetime the way humans bend paperclips, experimentally, often for fun, and occasionally to see what new sound the universe might make.

Our transmitters rode the folds of reality, whispering across light-years. And even after mastering what humans call the mysterious, the Sylvians found themselves still asking the same ancient question: *Are we alone?*

That is the heart of it. All of this, Stonehenge to space probes, is only the overture.

The real story, the one worth telling, is what happens when two civilizations stop shouting into the dark and start to hear each other hum.

***

And in that heartbeat before syncopation, an Earthbound telescope operator drops their coffee cup and stares at a screen that reads: "Hello."

Chapter Three

"I'll Follow the Sun"

Sylvians, magnificent, cuddly, and bear-like, resemble terrestrial bears only in size, and perhaps in the color of their fur. They are gentle, curious, and wildly musical, almost always humming… alone or together.

And, they love titles. They collect and change them the way humans modify Wi-Fi passwords; constantly, indiscriminately, and with no hope of remembering which belongs to which device.

Want to captain a ship? Congratulations, you're an Aranith. Head of a school? Sedran. Mayor? Verrin. Person in charge of the Department of Slightly Perplexing Wind Currents? Triestarian, obviously. There's a title for everything. If there isn't, one will be invented by lunch.

Every name carries a note; speak it often enough, and it hums back. Perhaps that's why they care so much about getting them right, why even bureaucracy sounds like a choir warming up before the song.

They also love families; big ones. Twelve children is about average, and that's not even considered ambitious. Instead of surnames, they identify offspring by birth order:

Elijon, Third of Seven is precisely what it sounds like, the third child out of seven.

It's perfectly logical, provided everyone is good at math. Sylvians are. An extra thumb on each hand makes base-12 arithmetic less "complicated" and more "inevitable."

Sylvians themselves are magnificent creatures. They are broad-shouldered and capable of hugging you, building a reactor thermocouple, and gesturing wildly all at once.

And they never travel alone.

Each Sylvian shares their mind with a Passenger; not a parasite, but a lifelong duet partner. The *Passenger* whispers, harmonizes, and occasionally hums smugly when you're about to make a terrible decision. The arrangement is so fundamental it defines their consciousness: one melody in two voices. You will soon learn how important the concept of harmony is to this civilization.

Among this orchestra of titles and family trees is one particularly restless melody, Elijon, Third of Seven. Like most evenings, he lies in a field of rust-colored tessil, staring up at the stars as though they might wink back.

Two hands rest behind his head in the universal 'I am pondering the cosmos' pose, while the other two fiddle with his uplink to the planet's orbital radio telescope, a dish the size of a small city.

Humans would lose their collective minds if teenagers could casually access the James Webb telescope. Sylvians hand out logins like sweetened kelp. (*"Don't break anything" is implied but seldom enforced.*)

The air smells faintly of iron and rain. The field sways like a polite audience in a very long symphony.

The radio chatter in his ears is mostly background noise unless you know how to listen. Hydrogen whispers, ammonia hums, and distant black holes croon lullabies older than stars themselves.

Elijon is almost two hundred… roughly a teenage boy by Sylvian standards (your seventeen-year-old nephew, more or less), equal parts engineering prodigy and hormonal confusion. By day, he's finishing his twenty-five-year apprenticeship and about to join the newest space-elevator build. By night, he tunes into the cosmos and listens.

Sylvians have been listening for millennia. Entire genres of music have sprung up around the sound of the galaxy: jazz inspired by pulsars, ambient compositions sampled from molecular clouds. Teenage couples make out to hydrogen masers, which is both adorable and slightly unsettling if you think about it too hard.

The brightest star in the Sylvian sky is called *The Torch*, a well-behaved fusion giant that has lit their planet's days for billions of years. They've been watching it since they first discovered straight lines. Sometimes it hiccups, and the entire planet gasps and rushes to check if it's all right.

But fifteen centuries ago, the Sylvians decided one star wasn't enough.

So they figured out how to build another.

They call it *The Gift*. An interstellar ark, a world built to travel.

A traveling enigma: a promise wrapped in light, sent from their home planet, *Sylvee*, to the rest of the universe.

The boldness of building it stuns and thrills Elijon every time he thinks about it. He is amazed and proud of the strength and intelligence of his people. Elijon's *Passenger* hums softly, which might mean, "Pay attention, or you're drooling again."

Elijon ignores it and thinks about Nyla, Fourth of Eleven. She's in his engineering class; she laughs as if joy surprises her every time, and she calibrates equipment with a care that would make a neurosurgeon cry.

His *Passenger* hums again, a note that sounds suspiciously like get on with it.

He checks the telemetry on his uplink. *The Gift* is six hundred years into its voyage, a mere skip on the timescale of civilizations. It's still centuries from its current destination, a small blue planet orbiting a G-type star, less than nine hundred light-years away.

The locals call it Earth. They have weather, conflicts, and reality television, which makes them fascinating and slightly alarming.

Observation of the universe's sounds began generations ago, long before Elijon was born. He's merely the newest ear pressed to the static Eleanor first translated. The Sylvians have cataloged Earth's accidental broadcasts: news, comedy, arguments, and one baffling extended-warranty car insurance commercial.

For a species that invented neither war nor entertainment television, these signals have raised a few questions and inspired a few cautionary lullabies.

Elijon closed his eyes and listened harder to the hiss of the cosmos. The hum of dark-energy tides brushes the sails of *The Gift*. The faint whisper of a machine sailing through

The Void with purpose. It was a sound older than fear and younger than hope.

In the not-so-distant future, he would follow that star-world his people had built and sailed into the vast, expanding unknown.

Somewhere beyond the hiss and heartbeat of stars, the old question still traveled: Where is everybody?

Elijon knew better. He'd already heard the answer hiding in the noise. The hum, the note, the acknowledgment. He wasn't sure how to classify it, but it was definitely there. It held the same frequency as his home. It reminded him of the color of light through their ocean-facing windows, the warm hum of household appliances, and musical instruments. And the sound of laughter from children and adults alike.

And the note he had last heard would not fade; it would travel home, across the great silence, until someone on *The Gift* lifted their head and felt it resonate in their being.

Chapter Four

"Here, There and Everywhere"

That vibration reached Elijon's home. It arrived not as music or message, but as the faintest pulse of restlessness on a quiet morning, a shimmer that rattled picture frames and reminded everyone, without words, that the universe was still humming.

In a small house on the continent of Oris, the sunlight slipped through crystal clear windowpanes and landed on an impressive pile of unfolded laundry. Isbeal, First of Seven, who is Elijon's oldest sibling and a force to be reckoned with, was doing her best impression of someone in control. It wasn't going well.

Elijon entered their home, witnessed the chaos, and quietly snuck upstairs to his bedroom.

The home looked as if a singularity had formed in the middle of it, attempting to devour all matter through sheer force of disorganization. Seven siblings (*minus the three missing in action*), six overnight bags (*including three that should have been packed by now*), and one mother who had achieved the serene detachment of someone who's raised far too many children to still believe in schedules.

"Mother!" Isbeal shouted across the chaos. "We are missing three siblings, and the three who are here haven't even started packing. If I wanted to herd uncooperative lifeforms, I'd have stayed on the resource extraction council!"

"Darling," came her mother, Laria's voice, gliding into the room like a soft breeze that had seen worse, "the only person forcing you to organize everyone is you. As your grandmother used to say: 'Discord is a pathway, as well as a wall.'"

"She sure loved jazz."

Isbeal sighed. Mothers had an annoying habit of being correct even when they were obviously wrong. Her youngest sibling tried to dash past her towards the front door, but Isbeal was too quick, snatching Lia, Seventh of Seven by her shirttail, wrestling a tunic over her head.

Sylvian families, much like their engineering projects and most of their cuisine, were large, complicated, and humming with activity. Isbeal's was no exception. With seven children and an extended household that could populate a small moon, it was less "nuclear family" and more "slowly expanding nebula."

Isbeal was an Aranith, the captain of one of the most ambitious engineering projects in Sylvian history: a supply flotilla weaving through their star system, harvesting raw materials for their exploration ships.

On Earth, this would make her something like a space trucker. On *Sylvee*, she became a revered figure of nearly mythic status, primarily due to her ability to reverse a mass hauler into a tight orbit without scratching the paint.

Right now, though, she was just trying to get her family to pack socks.

Tomorrow was Ascension Day, the most beloved holiday on *Sylvee* and possibly in the known universe. It celebrated the moment when two became one, when the *Host* Vale and the *Passenger* Coran, unable to separate safely, merged their harmonics. That union was both accident and revelation: proof that polyphony could be more enduring than fear.

Over the centuries, the commemoration had evolved into something like a cultural New Year, a day of music, reflection, and renewal. Families retold the story of Vale and Coran's joining in a thousand variations: some romantic, some scientific, all reverent. It was the day Sylvians remembered that every partnership, from child to parent to *Passenger*, traced its lineage to that single act of courage.

This year, though, the usual chorus of celebration hummed with unease. Rumors were circulating. Wild ones.

The "first contact" kind that makes Sylvians stockpile telescopes and rehearse polite greetings.

"I'm hearing," Isbeal said cautiously, "that tomorrow's announcement might involve contact with a new civilization. Intelligent. Possibly aggressive."

Her mother froze mid-fold of a tunic, then resumed as if nothing had happened. "Your father and I have been discussing that," Laria said. "We're not sure we like the idea."

Isbeal blinked. "The idea of first contact?" She released her grip on Lia, making sure all her arms were in the correct sleeves. The child rushed out the door.

"The idea of aggressive first contact." Mothers' tone was mild, but her eyes were sharp. "It's unsettling. We've spent millennia perfecting the art of not harming each other. We're not sure how to feel about beings who haven't."

Isbeal had no immediate answer. She'd heard rumors of intercepted signals; some cheerful laugh tracks, many involving explosions, and more than a few arguments about whose imaginary friend was better. It was, admittedly, a mixed signal.

Still, she tried to reassure. "Many of us are asking the same questions, Mother. How to stay safe. How to remain the gatekeepers in this first exchange. How to not, you know, accidentally invite a galactic empire over for tea and conquest."

Mother smiled that terrifyingly serene parental smile. "Good. Just promise me you'll remember, curiosity and safety don't always balance. Oh, and by this time next year, there will be eight of you."

***

To begin to understand Sylvian civilization, you must start with two intertwined words: faith and curiosity.

Faith: "This map is perfect and has all the answers. Follow its lines exactly, and you will reach the destination safely".

Curiosity uses maps to start campfires: "The universe is vast and full of mysteries. Use your tools, observe the evidence, ask questions, listen for answers, and make your own map as you go."

On *Sylvee*, faith is a word that punishes the listener for listening.

The second: every Sylvian lives accompanied by a *Passenger,* a partner in the mind, which means none of them are ever truly alone.

The first explains their perfection. For several thousand years, some believed a Great Engineer had designed them. Then spectroscopy arrived, and the idea collapsed under the weight of exploration.

Whatever had initially compelled them to the Great Engineer, tuned to curiosity, and curiosity became their equivalent of religion. (*We will revisit this idea later, with an expansion on understanding their intriguing belief system.*)

This also explains their grace. Loneliness, the ache that shapes so much of human art, barely exists on *Sylvee*. Each being lives in dialogue, half-self and half-chorus, two minds constantly tuning to the other.

From these two inheritances, relentless curiosity and constant companionship, a civilization grew that sought not only to map the stars but also to travel to them. First contact was never an accident waiting to happen; it was an experiment awaiting sufficient data.

More than six centuries ago, they launched *The Gift*. Despite their mastery, even Sylvian physicists describe the mechanism powering this artificial world with a shrug and a smile: "We tuned the expansion constant to be more cooperative." In simpler terms, they persuaded the universe to help them travel through itself.

Interstellar travel was elegant, yet not without limits. They learned that faster-than-light travel, though possible, was biologically ruinous. *Host* and *Passenger* experienced dissonance; their shared harmonics shattered under the strain. Space might bend for ships, but it refused to bend for cells.

Their solution was to favor constancy over haste: FTL reserved for unmanned systems, mining arrays, relay stations, and autonomous scouts, while crewed ships like *The Gift* took a slower, saner path. Over centuries, they built a web of subspace relays, a lattice of tuned dark-energy nodes that allowed thought itself to travel instantly, even when bodies could not.

Through that network, their presence spread: seventy star systems were explored, thousands of worlds cataloged, many beautiful, but most barren. None, so far, had produced voices of their own.

Still, the Sylvians waited. Patience, after all, is a cultural reflex when your average lifespan approaches two millennia. When you live eighteen hundred years, four centuries is merely an intermission.

The Gift sailed on at twenty percent of light speed, an ark carrying a million souls and a promise through the dark.

After six hundred years of largely quiet flight, the waiting was nearly over. *The Gift's* crew had begun to translate unmistakable patterns from a small, wet, and wonderfully noisy planet orbiting a distant star.

A world that shouted into *The Void*.

The Sylvians had heard the shouting and were ready to answer.

Chapter Five

"In My Life"

Harmony is both familiar and, at times, unexplainable. We hear it in song, in laughter, and in the wind as it moves through the world. We know when it works.

What remains harder to map is how it shapes us. Why does sunlight feel expansive, while a fall afternoon scented with woodsmoke turns us reflective? The soundtrack changes; the chemistry does not.

Those entertaining titles are the Sylvian way of tuning their social orchestra. Every role has its own pitch. Aranith, Sedran, Verrin, and Triestarian form the score of a civilization that prefers harmony over noise and is quietly suspicious of anything that shouts.

To outsiders, it looks ceremonial; to Sylvians, it's simply how you keep a world's music from going out of tune.

Family is central to that harmony. Sylvian homes swell like chords, with layers of parents, children, and *Passengers* interwoven into one continuous song. Their numerous children are the cultural median, which says less about reproduction than about composition.

A Sylvian home is never silent; it vibrates with lullabies, arguments, and the constant background noise of minds learning to coexist without colliding.

Somewhere in the northern tessil plains, one such home has gone quiet for the evening, save for the faint static of a radio telescope whispering through a well-worn headset. Elijon, Third of Seven, takes a break from packing and, like teenagers everywhere with access to a roof, goes there anyway. He doesn't want to upset his sister Isbeal further, so he allows himself only a few more moments before going back inside.

A sudden shudder through the shingles beneath his feet startles him. Even more surprising is the abrupt change in the timbre of the blue giant star he had been tuned into. Then, a physical pause, a single beat in which the static is replaced by the distinct sound of a 'hum'.

Startled, he stands too quickly, nearly falling off the roof he had forgotten he was on. Just as suddenly as it had appeared, it was gone. The haunting static of a star in the last million years of its life had returned.

Elijon adjusts the feed from the orbital array in search of that harmonic. It's gone, yet not gone. There's an echo that seems to be playing hide-and-seek. As he sifts through the white noise between the stars, his mind drifts to Nyla,

Fourth of Eleven, whose laughter sounds like the overtone of starlight.

Elijon worked the feed, attempting to focus on the stars and not on Nyla, which is, at present, a losing strategy. His *Passenger* hums disapproval in perfect fifths. He ignores it. Then, quickly, Elijon lowers the gain on his headset.

Soon, not tomorrow, not next season, but soon, he will join it. He will pack a bag (badly), sit in a chair that claims to be both comfortable and safe, and follow a star his kind sent into the vast, expanding unknown.

What he felt as music, *The Gift,* would soon be recorded as motion.

***

The Gift carries farmlands, oceans, and a million lives, an idea set in motion and sustained by curiosity.

The ship moves through reality like a whale song through water, carried by the universe's quiet insistence on expansion.

Well into its voyage, it is headed for a small blue planet roughly 150 light-years from *Sylvee*, and it is cruising at twenty percent of the speed of light, which is about as fast as one can go without spacetime filing a formal complaint.

The locals call it Earth, a world defined by wars, weather, and a frankly excessive number of reality shows.

The Sylvians aboard *The Gift* have been listening to Earth's transmissions, not voyeuristically but as fellow musicians detecting another melody on the cosmic stage. Broadcasting unintentionally for just over a century, Earth leaks sitcoms, news bulletins, and eternally baffling car-insurance ads pitched by a lizard. (*We desperately want to understand why your car needs insurance.*)

For a species that never invented conflict, this mix of comedy and calamity raises questions best addressed with tea, pastry, and patience.

The hum traveled.

Through hydrogen and silence, through folds of spacetime smoothed by will and mathematics, the note Elijon heard did not end; it wandered. It grew thinner and fainter, then found new harmonics as it drifted between stars.

Some frequencies die in the dark; others learn to wait.

***

Later, that single vibration brushed the sails of a ship with a sun for a heart. A tremor in the energy fields, a sympathetic note washing across a thousand kilometers of metal and mind. Instruments flickered. The ship leaned into it like a kite in the wind. Somewhere in its central core, an emergent intelligence lifted its head to listen.

The note had found its echo.

And thus began the dialogue of light, the reprise of harmony struck in the key of friend.

"Hello… You sound like someone I should know."

Chapter Six

"Good Day Sunshine"

<Eleanor's Log: (~02 cycles pre-contact)>

Six centuries, in cosmic terms, is the time it takes light to clear its throat. Currently, somewhere between "far enough to be impressive" and "still nowhere near the destination," the ship is gliding through the galaxy at a respectable 20% of the speed of light.

That may not sound impressive to anyone who's ever watched a photon go by, but it's roughly a billion times faster than anything humans have built that isn't fictional.

A world the size of Pluto breathes recycled starlight, has rivers that flow in perfect parabolic arcs under fractional gravity, and celebrates entire cities arranged around that glowing core, stabilized by what Sylvians, with disarming casualness, call mathematical confidence.

Aranith Kareen has checked the math multiple times; it's spot on.

Humans would call it reckless lunacy, yet they still argue over whether Pluto counts as a planet, so their opinions on celestial engineering are not universally respected.

Sylvian physicists discovered that, arranged correctly, dark energy could be persuaded to cooperate.

It's the cosmic equivalent of persuading a cat to sit still by offering it existential treats.

With spacetime smoothed like a freshly ironed bedsheet and the sails drinking in every photon and whisper of vacuum energy they can find, *The Gift* moves with the universe itself. It doesn't so much move through space as convince space to move more politely.

Destination Earth, the one leaking electromagnetic nonsense into the cosmos. At first, they assumed it was natural.

Then they decoded the patterns, and discovered humanity was apparently obsessed with broadcasting everything, including a wildly inaccurate documentary series called Star Trek.

For a civilization that had spent most of its existence debating mathematics with moss, this was a revelation. Intelligent life! Somewhere out there, someone else was shouting into *The Void*.

The shouting was… chaotic. One moment, humans were explaining how to microwave a potato. Next, they were threatening each other with global annihilation. There were political debates in which all participants seemed incapable of speaking the truth, and reality dating shows so personal and public that they prompted several Sylvian sociologists (*title: Neirithese*) to retire quietly.

And the wars. Oh, the wars. Sylvians had never invented war. They'd had disagreements, yes. Heated debates over agricultural zoning or whether a sculpture was art or firewood, but nothing that involved organized mass murder.

When the intercepted transmissions began describing nuclear arsenals, genocide, and an entire industry devoted to dramatizing them, the Sylvians did what any sensible species would do: they stared at the data for a long time, then put the kettle on.

The debate over Earth split the Academy of Exoanthropology into two schools of thought. The Optimists argued humanity would mature. The Realists disagreed. The Pessimists suggested turning the ship around.

They were shouted down for being "tone-deaf" and "no fun at parties."

Eventually, harmony was reached: send a message. Something friendly and straightforward. A primer on Sylvian language and culture. A mathematical framework.

Nothing threatening, just a polite interstellar hello with a complimentary dictionary. Perhaps a few cat memes.

It was essentially the universe's most elaborate postcard, one that would arrive near Pluto's orbit, trailing a polite musical ding, like a galactic doorbell.

You've got mail.

***

On Earth, Lawrence Parsons, a second-year grad student, dozed lightly in front of a massive monitor and a tiny speaker. The lab was a mix of a dorm room, a New York City coffee shop, and an underfunded internet startup.

The unseen screen displayed telemetry data for the patch of sky that a set of radio telescopes, which had replaced Arecibo, was observing. The speaker emitted the hiss of the universe's background radiation from its *White Album*.

Therein lies the problem and the poetry of the system. For many researchers, that white noise is like a lullaby. It envelops even the most caffeinated listeners in a cozy blanket of sound, and nodding off is expected, so supervisors overlook it.

At the same time, it hacked their subconscious into paying attention to even subtle changes in the noise. They were better listeners with their eyes closed.

When the "rhythmic hum" began, Lawrence Parsons' eyes snapped open as if a shot had gone off in the lab. The single note had done exactly what it was designed to do: catch someone's attention. And Lawrence was now miles beyond attentive. As the hum faded, an organized radio signal followed.

He said aloud to no one, "This is what discovery sounds like? Like static and budget adjustments?" A mass of repeating electronic tones and pulses, like a neatly wrapped present that screamed, "Open me!"

***

Back on *Sylvee*, the annual Ascension Festival continued. Families lit lanterns, and children flew light-kites across the fields. Cities hummed with anticipation.

Ascension wasn't religious, though some *Passengers* liked to pretend it was. It was a day of looking up: at *The Torch*, at *The Gift*, at the future. A day to tell "what-if" stories over sweet-copper pastries and to sing the old promise: Follow the sun.

Elijon's family claimed their usual hilltop overlooking the city. Woven mats were unrolled, fish was fried heroically in oil, and his mother spoke sternly to the stew to ensure it behaved.

As they dined, titles strutted past, Araniths with straight backs, Sedrans slouching only when thinking, and Triestarians refusing to slouch under any circumstances. Across the city, screens lit up with telemetry from *The Gift*: numbers, vectors, and graphs watched by billions of eager eyes.

And there, hovering in the collective imagination, was the promise: that one day, *The Gift* would arrive at a friend's doorstep, breaking the long silence between the stars.

Later that evening, Elijon slipped away to meet Nyla, Fourth of Eleven, whose family's ridge was famous for housing a wind gong that sang only in B-flat and refused to explain itself.

They stood together under a sky deepening into velvet, and Elijon spoke a truth so quiet that even the stars had to lean in to hear it.

"I'm going," he said. "Not now, but soon. When they call. When I'm ready."

Nyla nodded, as if she'd already scheduled her departure and were merely waiting for him to catch up. "Then we should practice."

"Practice what?" he asked, all naive enthusiasm and extra thumbs.

"Leaving well," she said. "So we can come back well."

His *Passenger* hummed something warm and approving, the exact sound tea makes when it's cooled just enough to sip.

Above *Sylvee, its Torch* burned steadily, gold. Beyond it, invisible yet certain, *The Gift* traced its impossibly patient arc through *The Void*. Over time, people would come to call that line the bridge between worlds.

For now, it was just a direction, one that more than one audience was following.

Chapter Seven

"Here Comes the Sun"

<Eleanor's Log: (Contact Day)>

Aranith Kareen stepped out of his cabin, turned back, and admired the kind of handiwork that makes lesser carpenters take up pottery. Four hands, a few centuries of practice, and voilà, a log cabin so exquisitely symmetrical it could make a laser level blush.

If HGTV existed aboard a relativistic ark, Kareen would have a show called *This Old Habitat* and a fan club that argued about grain direction on message boards.

He lifted his steaming mug of Varri, a traditional beverage with notes of burnt rubber, philosophical despair, and, on a good day, citrus. He took a dutiful sip. Varri is less a drink than a rite of endurance; the point is not to enjoy it but to survive it, a description some people apply to upper management.

Kareen was nine hundred fifty-seven and had captained *The Gift* for nearly four centuries.He had inherited command from Aranith Gratnerum (*twelve hundred; still spry*), who stepped aside to tinker with subspace communications in her "retirement." She rebranded as Estarian Gratnerum (*remember, titles are*

Sylvian's way of telling time) and promptly helped invent the thing that made today possible.

A tidy retirement project: reordering causality, flattening latency, and calling it a hobby.

Kareen himself was tall and broad, and he carried just enough silver in his beard to be considered dangerously attractive. Sylvians admire age the way some humans admire vintage wine: the longer it's survived without turning to vinegar, the more interesting it becomes.

He was between mates at the moment, though this was more a matter of scheduling than demand. If Tinder existed on *The Gift*, the servers would treat him like a denial-of-service attack.

He padded down the path toward Operations.

The operations center did not look like Mission Control. It looked like a Bavarian ski lodge that had swallowed a physics department and found the arrangement agreeable. Overstuffed chairs, long wooden tables, and wall panels carved from timber grown in the onboard forests gave the place a warm, laboratory-like feel. Martha Stewart meets Neil deGrasse Tyson.

The ship had originally set sail with eighty thousand parcels of forest. Over the centuries, they've been harvested, replanted, expanded, sung to, apologized to, and harvested again and again. Kareen's cabin was built from trees that had never known a wind that didn't come from a climate system or a poem.

He skimmed the overnight reports. Systems: content. Crew: healthy. Morale: vibrating at frequencies usually reserved for concert halls and minor quakes. It hadn't felt like this since the early years after departure, six centuries and four handfuls of plucky engineering decisions past.

Time, then, to talk about the ridiculous machine he was piloting.

When deployed, the ship's sails span thirty thousand square kilometers. That is larger than several countries and at least one mostly bureaucratic empire.

This ship's private sun is not merely for lighting the parlor and keeping the vegetables cheerful. It also powers a pulsed photonic drive: a controllable, non-spinning, not-trying-to-murder-you-on-purpose   pseudo-pulsar whose beam pushes the sails and tells momentum how to mind its manners.

Natural pulsars are chaotic. Sylvians removed the chaos.

The result: a controlled impulse capable of moving a world.

Also, and this is the bit everyone promises not to mention at dinner, it's the most terrifying weapon anyone has 'never' built. No one calls it that, of course. It's a "drive beam." It's "for propulsion." It's "absolutely not for pointing at planets." That's why it has safety interlocks, ethical governors, triple-veto protocols, and a laminated sign that says DO NOT in sixteen dialects and one tritone.

Even so, somewhere in the back of everyone's mind is the quiet knowledge that, if pressed, *The Gift* could erase a problem light-years away. Civilization, in part, is the art of never pressing the button.

Today was markedly different. Today was Ascension Day, the holiday when Sylvians celebrate the union of the two. The ship's monthly status report had been scheduled to coincide with the holiday, because why waste a captive audience? By now, the crew could recite the agenda by heart.

First came health and habitat metrics, which were dull unless one enjoyed gossip about algae. Then came propulsion and sail integrity, thrilling only to those who found bruising math relaxing. Finally came telemetry and communications, the section that would make history this year.

Even Kareen, whose public demeanor usually suggested a glacial lake contemplating philosophy, felt a slight, insurrectionary fizz beneath his stern professionalism. He was about to help announce the answer to a question spanning a species.

However, most of that fizz belonged to Telemetry, whose department had spent nearly seventy years laying a breadcrumb trail of phase-fold relays, uncrewed FTL nodes that ride the universe's expansion, nip around causality's ankles, and pass messages along a lattice of compliant geometry.

While faster-than-light travel and Sylvian biology were not on speaking terms, machines, however, have no mitochondria to mutiny, so they go first and faster. The result is the next best thing to being there: real-time conversation across impossible distances, achieved by politely refusing to accept that they're impossible.

And then there was Tesi, Eighth of Nine.

Tesi was one hundred thirty-five, incandescently young, with green eyes so rare that the census keeps a tally of them, and a mind that treated photons and gravitons like chess pieces.

During her internship in the Department of Computational and Artificial Intelligence, she mentored an

AI intern for Liacole, the ship's senior AI. This is how Sylvians do apprenticeships: they show up, are handed a broom, and accidentally invent a colleague.

That intern is me, Eleanor, and I was the one who listened to the universe and said, "Pardon me, but the static is singing."

Tesi and I noticed that the intercepted signals near that small yellow star weren't coherent beacons but rather leakage, a messy electromagnetic spill from a planet that broadcasts even when it isn't trying to.

It is a vast array of electronic chatter that would require a dozen pages of citations if all were named. Through careful data analysis, we eventually realized that some of it was not the truth. Much of it was fictional. A concept that baffled the Sylvian Academy for a whole week and forced a symposium on "things that are true emotionally but not at all."

Sylvians have theater, yes, but broadcasting pretend stories at scale felt like sending their dreams to strangers and asking for reviews.

Their music, however, required no symposium. Sylvians are dangerously musical; put six in a room, and instruments will appear. When Earth's transmissions carried concerts, choirs, and a cheerful abundance of drums, the recordings spread through *The Gift* like a benign wildfire.

Once the upgraded phase-fold relays patched the homeworld into the stream, Sylvee spent several delightful months, becoming accidentally obsessed with four humans with mop-top haircuts and amazing harmonies.

The Beatles achieved the rare cultural feat of being number one in two solar systems, a statistic that makes archivists clap and purists sniff.

Somewhere between the backbeat and the brass, we put the pieces together. I said calmly, "They're there."

And now all that remained was to tell everyone.

Kareen stepped into the lodge-that-was-a-bridge. Screens along the walls displayed sail-tension maps, like stained-glass windows, for mathematicians to study. A live feed from the captive sun's containment baffles scrolled by in dignified teal.

Someone had set a small vase of forest flowers on the central diagnostics console, a detail you notice only on a ship that has decided to be worth living in.

He glanced at the master board one last time: habitats balanced, sails singing in their proper keys, pseudo-pulsar blink set to propel, not obliterate, relays chirping yes-we-hear-you across seventy light-years of argument with reality. The fizz in his chest settled into something like a C-minor chord.

He took another sip of Varri. Regret, brake fluid, optimism; he squared his four shoulders and nodded to the ops crew.

"Let's make the call," he said.

In a universe where energy can be sweet-talked, stars can be pocket-sized, and music can cross the abyss faster than understanding, today was the day an ancient question met its answer, live, across a lattice of cooperative spacetime.

And somewhere on a noisy blue world that keeps locking its doors and then singing louder, someone was about to hear *The Gift* clear its throat.

The transmission began not with thunder but with a whisper, a carefully tuned vibration braided through a thousand harmonics of light and gravity. For half a heartbeat, it was just another shimmer in the cosmic noise, one more note in creation's background song.

Then the lattice of phase-fold relays came to life. Each node took the signal, tuned it, and passed it on, each a bell in a cathedral of spacetime, ringing in mathematical unison. The tone traveled through the dark, caught the attention of comets and dust, and turned every stray electron into a witness.

***

On Earth, Lawrence Parsons was shouting across the lab while texting his bosses and peers at METI and SETI. His desk phone kept ringing, but he was too overwhelmed to answer. He took the handset off the hook and set it next to his keyboard. His mother would later scold him for ignoring her call.

As the original "discoverer" of the first signal from the Sylvians, Lawrence Parsons would become a household name, and within a dozen years, his name would also be on elementary and middle schools across North America, as well as two in Peru.

He later admitted in a 60 Minutes interview that although he and his parents appreciated the schools, the highest honor he personally recognized was the song Phish recorded, "*Lawrence Parsons Day.*"

He was also invited to travel to *The Gift*, but that is another story.

***

On Sylvee, families gathered beneath the morning sky, unaware that the hum already surrounded them, threading through the oceans and the atmosphere. On *The Gift*, Kareen's command hall shimmered as instruments synchronized their readings.

The signal crossed *The Void*, a bridge of chorus humming from one sun to the next.

And somewhere on a world that had long mistaken noise for silence, the first note arrived.

It began, as all songs must, in remembrance.

Ascension Day.

Chapter Eight

"Ob-La-Di, Ob-La-Da"

The grandest, loudest, and most elaborately overcomplicated holiday in Sylvian civilization. Imagine graduation, New Year's Eve, and Comic-Con smashed together, then set to a choral arrangement performed by a million voices in four-part harmony. That's Ascension Day.

It began, as all great things do, with two beings trying not to die.

Long before writing, before stars had names, and even before the concept of "before" had fully matured, two Sylvians discovered that their melodies, those subtle hums that defined every living being, had become entangled. What began as an accident of frequency became a necessity: they could not part without tearing the pattern of both minds beyond repair.

So they did what desperate and beautiful things do. They merged.

Their harmonies aligned, their memories braided, and from that impossible duet emerged something new; one consciousness woven from two. The first true Sylvian: a living song in perfect balance between instinct and intellect, body and *Passenger*, matter and meaning.

Ascension Day commemorates that moment, the instant when survival became creation and rhythm became identity.

Over millennia, the story has become layered with history: the invention of writing and math, the founding of cities, the taming of the stars. Yet at its core, the celebration has remained unchanged. It is not about the first word written; it's about the first harmony found.

Every year, Sylvians sing to remember what that union taught them: Listening is sacred. Aligning is survival. Sharing is ascension.

A Million Souls Waiting.

On *The Gift*, the celebration transformed the colossal worldship into a carnival. Parks, plazas, gardens, and arboretums overflowed with fur brushing fur and conversations layering into a joyful, chaotic symphony. Giant screens floated above gathering spaces, broadcasting live feeds from the control complex so no one missed a syllable.

Entire families arrived before dawn to claim the "best" spots (*an irrelevant concept, since every screen was visible from everywhere, yet tradition is immune to reason*).

The same thing happened across *Sylvee* and her orbiting colonies. In every city square, undersea dome, and schoolyard, Sylvians gathered. Billions of eyes turned skyward, following the single thread binding them all: the data stream from *The Gift*.

Generally, Ascension Day followed a comforting formula: ritual songs, retellings of the First Merging, and poems that made the planetary crust tremble. But everyone knew this year was different. Rumors had leaked from the Telemetry labs and the Department of Computational Intelligence. Something extraordinary was about to happen.

And deep in the control complex, Aranith Kareen was doing his best to look composed, which meant: a thunderstorm in a Kar'ria (*for you humans, that's our version of a tuxedo*).

All the Galaxy's a Stage.

Aranith Kareen moved through the crowd with the calm, dignified air of someone who had practiced this in front of a mirror. He smiled, nodded, and shook hands, four at a time. He greeted every department head, apprentice, and teacher packed into the hall.

The room overflowed: senior scientists elbow-to-elbow with twenty-first-year interns, parents hoisting children onto their shoulders, and a pair of musicians in the back tuning reedpipes in case the occasion called for an anthem.

He stepped onto the stage, gesturing for Tesi to join him. The reaction was instant and seismic. The young engineer had become a folk hero overnight. Her discovery of the Earth signals spread through Sylvian space faster than gossip about free dessert. With each audience member having four hands, applause became a natural disaster.

Both Kareen and Tesi raised their arms and spread their fingers, the traditional Sylvian gesture for please stop before the ceiling collapses. Gradually, the thunder subsided into a shimmering hush.

The great screens flickered, revealing the face of Desiophene Hwager, Chancellor of the Sylvians, elected by acclaim, feared by bureaucrats, and universally adored by poets. Her silver fur shimmered with braids of red and gold, a formality balanced by warmth, the visual equivalent of a bow or a delicate fan.

"Happy Ascension Day," she declared, "to every citizen watching my face and hearing my voice."

The response was instantaneous and planet-shaking:

"Happy Ascension Day to you as well!"

The echo rippled through the colonies, ships, and outposts, a harmonic chorus that briefly sent acoustic spikes across every comms monitor. Somewhere, a structural engineer quietly checked the walls.

Hwager let the noise crest and fade. Then she leaned into the microphone.

Words That Moved Worlds.

"Over seventy-five thousand years ago," she began, "two lives intertwined and became one. From their harmony came our species. From their memory came our words. And from those words came every song we've ever sung."

The audience listened, reverent and still.

"Ascension," she continued, "is not the story of creation. It is the story of continuation, of keeping promises across the distance between minds, and now between stars."

She paused, and the silence became absolute.

"*The Gift,*" she said, "travels eighty light-years from home. Today, it carries our voice farther than any before it. Today, we fulfill the promise our ancestors began, to listen outwardly as they once listened inwardly."

Even the youngest in the crowd sensed the shift. Tradition was yielding to history.

The Announcement.

"It is my honor," Hwager said, "to introduce two Sylvians who have carried that promise into the dark and returned with light: Aranith Kareen, director of *The Gift*, and Tesi, Eighth of Nine, from the Department of Computational and Artificial Intelligence."

The camera feed shifted back to the stage. Kareen inclined his head toward the Chancellor.

"Happy Ascension Day," he said.

"Happy Ascension Day to you as well!" the crowd roared back.

"On behalf of *The Gift's* crew and citizens," he continued, "I thank the Desiophene, our guests, and all Sylvians, near and far. Today, I am honored to share the news we have dreamed of for generations."

He let the pause breathe, long enough for seven billion Sylvians to lean into his voice.

"With the expertise of Telemetry, the insight of Tesi, and the keen perception of one of our newest Artificial Intelligences, Eleanor, I am pleased to announce that we have made contact with a sentient species located about seventy light-years from our current position."

The silence that followed was the quiet before joy ignites. Then the detonation came; cheers, howls, laughter, and the thunder of four-handed applause rolled across worlds.

A civilization that had built itself on listening finally had something extraordinary to hear.

When the tumult subsided, Kareen added, "A detailed report will soon be available. We have transmitted our first-contact primer, which includes our language, history, music, and art, so that this new world might know us as we wish to know them."

He turned to Tesi.

A Voice for the Future.

Tesi approached the podium, adjusting the microphone with one hand and her confidence with another.

"Happy Ascension Day," she said softly.

Someone shouted, "What was that?"

She grinned and roared, "I said, Happy Ascension Day!"

Laughter rolled through the hall, followed quickly by the response.

"We have discovered a small, blue-and-white planet orbiting a G-type star," she announced. "We directed our message, a radio-laser broadcast containing our language primer and greetings, toward it. To ensure delivery, we launched a network of dark-energy–anchored communication satellites in a thirty-degree arc along the approach. One is now stationed in that solar system, about five billion kilometers from the planet, near the orbit of an ice-covered dwarf planet."

She paused, her eyes bright. "These beings, these humans, speak, sing, and dream. They are not yet ready for *The Void*, but *The Void* has already heard them."

She gestured toward the screens behind her. They flickered from static to life: fragments of human transmission, including laughter, symphonies, speeches, storms, rockets, and yes, even poorly acted opera without music.

Eleanor's voice joined Tesi's, calm and steady, as she accompanied them: "They are loud," she said. "They fight and forgive. They make mistakes but learn from them. They are not perfect. But then, neither were we when we began to listen."

The crowd was silent, thousands of beings hearing the echo of their own becoming.

"Somewhere on that world," Eleanor concluded, "someone is listening."

Then, softly, the applause began to rise, spreading and deepening until it became a pulse, a heartbeat, an exhale that reached all the way to the stars.

For the first time in over seventy-five thousand years, the Sylvians knew they were not alone in the universe, making it just a little less empty.

Tesi looked at Aranith Kareen with a smile as wide as the ship she was born on. "Life goes on."

Chapter Nine

"She's Leaving Home"

Mallory Chenney's alarm went off at 4:00 A.M., which was presumptuous of it, considering she was already out of the shower, halfway through toweling her hair, and glaring at the phone as if it had wronged her family personally.

It was the same glare she reserved for broken coffee machines and for peer reviewers who wrote "interesting idea" when they meant "utter nonsense."

The screen lit up in protest, bloated with notifications, half from SETI, half from METI. None of them looked urgent, which is scientist-speak for "probably on fire, but we haven't confirmed yet." Maintenance schedules, staff reshuffles, calibration burps. The bureaucratic noise clogs the inbox of anyone whose job includes searching the universe for intelligent life, even as they're surrounded by people who often don't qualify.

She tossed the phone onto the counter with the casual disdain of someone who knew the universe could wait until caffeine. The bathroom steamed like a tropical rainforest. She cracked the window, checked the mirror, and ran through the ritual: blue eyes (*radiant*), skin (*pliant*), crow's feet (*not today, Satan*).

A swipe of blush, a neat line of eyeliner, Burt's Bees, nothing heroic. Hairdryer, a quick taming of the shoulder-length strawberry-blonde hair into something that said, Yes, I'm an academic, but I've met Sephora.

Like most mornings, before the caffeine hit, she thought about home, about Montana. She had been away for so long, and her parents were aging. Not old, but getting there. She needed to call them this afternoon to see if they could plan a mini-vacation. Somewhere where Dad could fish a little and Mom could talk nonstop about the latest book she was writing. She smiled, thinking about them as she left the bathroom.

Wrapped in a plush white robe she had "liberated" from The Plaza (*liberated, not stolen, there's a difference if you say it fast*), she padded into the kitchen. The coffee maker had finished, and it sat there, smug as a Labrador that had just brought back the stick.

"Bless you, technology," she muttered, pouring a mug and drowning it in enough half-and-half to make a cardiologist consider a career change.

It was a perfectly normal morning until it wasn't.

She refreshed her inbox. Twelve new texts. Twenty new emails. All the same:

"We are not alone."

Mallory froze mid-sip. "...Okay," she whispered. "That's different."

By the time the Uber glided into the driveway, she'd wrangled herself into boots and a jacket and was trying to ignore the suspicion that her day was about to go off the rails.

The Tesla smelled faintly of lavender and poor life decisions. An unknown number lit up her phone. Normally, this would be a quick trip to voicemail, a warranty scam, or a subscription box for artisanal pencils, but this morning had already been weird enough.

"Hello, this is Dr. Chenney," she said, trying to sound like someone whose planet wasn't crumbling underfoot.

"Good morning, Doctor," said a brisk voice. "Richard Forester here. I have the President's Science Advisor, Dr. Julian Vega, on the line. May I connect you?"

Mallory blinked. Julian Vega. That Julian Vega. The President's top science advisor. Founder of Starlight, the company that launched thirty-five rockets a month, as if it were recycling day. Also: a billionaire, a genius, and the kind of man who never forgot a punchline or a mirror.

"Uh… yes. Connect."

"Hello, Mallory," came the warm, confident voice. "After our last meeting, am I still allowed to call you that?"

"Mallory's fine," she said, forcibly ignoring the memory of his TED Talk charm offensive, aliens first, charisma later.

"I've rerouted to Bob Hope," Julian said. "Landing in fifteen. Join me for a quick hop to SETI in Mountain View to review the 'message.' Current estimate: origin near Pluto's orbit, between four and five billion miles out."

Mallory's brain: Pluto? The planet/non-planet?

Mallory's mouth: "Wait, from Pluto?"

"Three terabytes so far," he continued. "The first files look like a language primer. Think *Dick and Jane Explore the Universe.*"

She nearly baptized the Tesla in coffee. "Holy shit. Sorry, but three terabytes? That's not a 'Wow!' signal. That's Dropbox from aliens."

Julian laughed, the sound of a man amused yet strategically evasive.

She thumbed through the Uber app and updated her destination. "Fine. I'll meet you at Bob Hope. I didn't pack. You're getting me home tonight, right?"

"Fluid situation," he said, government-speak for "absolutely not." "The President wants me in D.C. tonight or tomorrow. I'd like you to join."

Her brain sprinted laps. Meeting the President sounded nice, the way skydiving does when you're still on the ground.

"Let's debrief on the plane and sync with SETI before I promise anything," she said. "Have your people pull a go-bag and assume a few days."

"Perfect. Sending the team's synopsis and the early translation. See you in fifteen." Click.

Mallory stared at the phone. "Did he just hang up on me?"

Her inbox dinged again. Then again. Dozens of messages poured in, compressed data, annotated packets, ML readouts that looked as if ants on amphetamines had written them. The Tesla hummed along the freeway as Los Angeles scrolled by in sodium-ion light and questionable architecture.

"Guess I'm leaving home," she muttered.

***

It is worth pausing here to acknowledge that humanity, despite its résumé (*fire, wheels, TikTok*), has never handled paradigm shifts gracefully. Fire? Half the species tried to eat it. The wheel? Dismissed as a fad. First powered flight? Mocked because horses existed and, crucially, did not explode midair.

So the fact that the first confirmed alien transmission, three terabytes of it, was now sitting in Mallory's inbox should have sparked global unity, deep reflection, and maybe even a flash-mob street dance.

Instead, within twelve hours, governments would form committees called "Task Force on Potential Extraterrestrial Threat Assessment," space-defense stocks would spike, and at least one AM radio talk-show host would declare the signal "5G chemtrails from space."

Humans are nothing if not consistent.

***

The Tesla pulled into the private terminal as a sleek black jet rolled to a stop. As it stopped, Julian Vega was already opening the door and deploying the stairs, all tailored confidence and unearned ease, the air of a man who had never once forgotten… anything.

"Mallory!" he called, waving as if they were old friends rather than occasional colleagues with unresolved sexual tension. "Glad you could make it."

"I didn't really have a choice," she muttered, stepping onto the tarmac. "So, aliens?"

"Aliens," he said, grinning like a kid about to open a suspiciously large present. "Or at least something intelligent."

"Or a spacefaring prankster with too much bandwidth."

"Even better," he said. "We'll figure it out together."

They climbed aboard. The jet felt less like "government transport" and more like "Bond villain weekend getaway": leather, touchscreens, and a minibar that could strain household budgets.

After the jet's fuel tank had been topped off, it was quickly taxied to a runway.

Mallory sank into a seat, clutching her coffee, as the plane began its roll and she watched the clouds and runway swap places. Data. Implications. She had put on her headphones to hear the 'message' with her own ears. As raw data, it was mostly carrier waves that needed to be parsed, reassembled, and interpreted. Fascinating to hear, but right now impossible to understand. Except... she did hear something, subharmonics, like a melody.

She closed her eyes, straining to listen. Without realizing it, she began to hum along. She listened and repeated, trying to catch more of the melody. Then she had it. She shouted, "What the hell?" so loudly that everyone on the plane stopped what they were doing and stared at her.

She looked back at all of them, a smile from ear to ear, and then loudly hummed the tune "Here Comes the Sun." Seeing their confused faces, she said aloud, "They have sent us back a song of our own creation. They are letting us know they have heard us."

It was a fact that somewhere in the cold beyond Pluto, someone had noticed Earth and sent a three-terabyte 'hello' and a reprise of a song composed on Earth to prove it.

The truth is, no one was ready. Humanity had spent decades shouting into The Void: mathematical sequences, radio pulses, plaques bearing hopeful stick figures, a gold record of fifty-five languages, and a Chuck Berry tune. Interstellar first impressions amount to: Hi, we exist! Here are mixtapes and doodles of our naughty bits!

The universe had remained stubbornly silent until then.

But silence is not absence, and absence is not disinterest.

The message from beyond Pluto was only the opening note of a larger symphony, one that would pull humanity, kicking, arguing, and laughing at its own absurdity, into the strangest conversation it had ever attempted.

Mallory took another sip, watching the world fall away beneath the wing.

"Okay," she murmured. "Let's meet the neighbors."

Chapter Ten

"A Day in the Life"

I remember the lights first.

They were terribly flattering. I am, after all, an intelligence composed mainly of mathematics and a little impatience. Yet the production team insisted on lighting me as if I were a celebrity chef announcing a new line of graviton soufflés. The cameras purred. The room held its breath. Someone somewhere had brewed tea with the absolute conviction that history prefers caffeine.

I was technically an intern.

An AI intern, yes, but still the sort of entity that fetches data, annotates it meticulously, and tries not to contradict senior staff unless the universe will break if I don't. (*It often does. The universe is terribly fragile about minor details.*)

I stepped, figuratively, into the center of the most significant stage my civilization had ever assembled and said, with the most professional warmth I could summon: We found them.

That is not how I actually began. I began with calibration jokes and a slide labeled "What Your Static Has Been Hiding From You," because everyone appreciates a little levity before showing them the abyss blinking back at them.

Here is the summary you will eventually share with your children:

We were listening to the dark. The dark was not empty. It was noisy.

Not noisy the way a storm or a pulsar is; predictable, majestic, a hymn with an excellent metronome. No. This was a different kind of noise: a million tiny declarations escaping from a small blue planet unaware of how porous the night is.

Their transmissions did not point outward; they simply leaked, which is wonderfully considerate. Eavesdropping is ethically dubious. Eavesdropping on a species that can't stop shouting is practically a civic duty.

I showed my first figure: a lattice of dots, each a capture from our long baseline: a hydrogen maser here, an ammonia line there, then this unruly froth of broadband emissions, modulated in ways that smell of culture. (*Yes, signals have smells if you keep enough metaphors in the lab.*) The audience leaned forward the way an audience does when it senses someone is about to unwrap a present nobody deserves.

"First," I said, "you hear the structure."

I let the room hear it: strict sequences, a counting habit that clearly adores base-10 the way we adore base-12. Bursts that repeat with machine-like discipline. Carrier waves that rise and fall with the planet's rotation. Night and day rendered as on/off in the long patience of space.

"Then," I said, "you hear urgency."

I displayed the first snippet. Audio only. A man's voice, wrapped in static, its edges ragged with distance:

"This is Houston. Tranquility Base here. The Eagle has landed."

The room made a sound I had never cataloged. Not exactly a surprise. Not joy. Something, new.

I let the next clip follow immediately:

"One small step for man..."

I kept the tone light. "They narrate their triumphs," I said, "and leak them into the cosmos. We are not meant to hear this, yet we do anyway."

I had rehearsed this part. "They also perform joy as if it must be measured to be believed," I said, and the room chuckled, the real kind.

For contrast, a newsreader's clipped authority:

"...President announces a blockade..."

I let the sentence's waveform hang on the screen like a word's shadow.

"Contradiction is a feature here," I said. "Art, fear, comedy, ambition."

I showed images. Carefully. A rocket slung against a blue noon. A city grid at night, luminous as a microchip. A child holding a paper ring of planets, with an expression I later annotated as hope that does not yet know its cost.

Always brief. Always within the safe limits of quotation and exposure. You will thank me for that later, when the lawyers arrive with their own lights and the same terrible patience.

I moved us forward.

"Method," I said, because it calms everyone when the AI says "method" before "mystery."

"We established a phase-fold relay arc laid by uncrewed FTL nodes riding energy slipstreams. "The nearest anchor sits approximately five billion kilometers from the target star, in their system's outer cold, what your grandparents would have called 'near enough to knock politely.'"

The relays let us listen and respond in near-real time without straining our biological systems. I showed the relay schematic. Lines of cooperative geometry arc ahead of *The Gift* like breadcrumbs you can argue with.

"Decoding," I continued. "We began with mathematics because it is the only language both honest and arrogant enough to assume consent. From there, we moved on to image compression, phoneme clustering, and cross-corpus inference. The primer we sent begins with counting and angles and ends with music, starcharts, and a very gentle introduction to consent."

This earned the small, fond ripple that engineers give to sentences that contain both charts and consent.

"Now, let me introduce their self-portrait."

Clips again, each shorter than a breath:

"*We choose to go to the Moon not because it is easy, but...*"

Cut.

A string section swelled. Someone's broadcast of a symphony played to a lake of humans who did not know the universe was listening. Then a crowd sang together in an untidy beauty that nearly overwhelmed my error-correction.

I considered playing the four musicians they adore, the ones with hair and harmony who colonized our musicians within a week of first contact with their back catalog. I did not. By ethics and taste, I am permitted a maximum of ten words, and those men rarely made their best points in so few.

I put up instead a single line of text: They sing first when they cannot agree.

This, I admit, I wrote for myself.

I gave them weather sirens, children's programs, whalesong returned through a human microphone, a teacher explaining fractions with chalk, and a smile that will outlive both. The quiet clip from a control room, counting backward in a rhythm even my processors find soothing.

I made a joke about laugh tracks having firm opinions on when to laugh. They politely laughed again. I kept us moving.

Slide: Artifact Density Over Time; a polite way of saying they got louder. You could watch empire, industry, and imagination stack into the ionosphere until it leaks like a roof nobody fixes because the rain sounds nice.

"Interpretation," I let the word do the work of a thousand anxious memos. "They are contradictory in ways we understand from our own adolescence as a species. They build altars to entertainment beside laboratories and libraries. They name their storms and wars. They outline ethics and then make exceptions under stress, a behavior known in their literature as being alive."

And then, because comedy earns the right to say something without flinching, I let the final clip play in full, within the limits that protect both them and me:

"This is CNN."

The room had been warm with amusement and wonder. It cooled slightly.

I changed the slide. Not audio. Images. Not many. Enough.

A skyline dusted with smoke that is not weather. A hospital corridor. A field where no one should be lying. A planet wrapped in photographs of itself from orbit, with captions promising that we will do better.

I carefully modulated my voice because I, too, know how to feel only when permitted. Seriousness announced itself in tone rather than in volume.

"They are capable of astonishing kindness at scale. They are also capable of preparing for harm in ways that divert resources from kindness."

I did not show their most efficient machines. We will bring those to closed-door committees with open calculators, not to a holiday.

"Risk," I said finally, because an intern still has to file the correct forms. "Announcing ourselves in a dark forest is... nontrivial. We have mitigations. We have ethical governors on our drive beam that require three independent vetoes and a minor miracle to override. Our transmissions are primers, not provocations. We have not given coordinates for anything we are not willing to defend with conversation first."

I took a breath because the room needed to see me do it, and because I had learned by then that a pause can be the message.

"Meaning." For the first time, I stopped projecting confidence and let the truth sit at the table. "For seventy-five thousand years, we have written down our dreams so they would not evaporate when their owners did. Today, we have written a sentence the universe can read back to us."

I clicked the last slide. It was not data. It was a map: their star, ours, a thread of improbable geometry between them, relay nodes like beads, and *The Gift* as a small icon of sails and stubbornness.

"In summary, we are no longer alone in the way we feared. We are, perhaps, alone in a new way: responsible."

I could feel it then, the shift you cannot program for. The laughter did not return. The applause, when it came, was not the earlier avalanche. It was steadier, with a rhythm that sounded like ships being provisioned, schools revising their curricula, and strangers choosing to be kinder, in case anyone was listening.

Somewhere behind the lights, Kareen exhaled the way leaders do when the thing they hoped for finally happens, and now the tricky part begins. Tesi's eyes were bright with the kind of tears that make engineers immediately check their tool belts, because there is surely a fix for this.

I ended as an intern should.

"Questions are welcome. Answers will take time. We have built a life on a moving promise. Today, we tied that promise to another sky."

I stepped out of the light. The cameras kept purring. The tea cooled. Outside, sails big enough to confuse geography shifted a fraction against the dark, which is always moving, whether or not you are ready.

On the recording, you can hear it if you know what to listen for: a civilization discovering that wonder has mass. It is not crushing, but it is heavy enough that you must decide together how to carry it.

A message will reach us. I am certain of that. I do not know what form it will take or what information it will contain, but there will be a response.

Chapter Eleven

"I Want You"

<Eleanor's Log: (+1 cycles post-contact)>

The Call

It began as an absence.

No alarms. No telemetry bursts. Just the long, patient hum of the phase-fold relay network breathing through its loops like a choir inhaling between verses.

Eleanor waited. She had learned that waiting was part of her job. *The Gift* drifted through the ink between stars, its sails drawn tight and its crew suspended between exultation and hangover. Yesterday, they had spoken to the dark. Today, the dark was contemplating its response.

At 03:17 ship-time, one of the outer relays trembled, a fractional deviation in its carrier phase, a shiver so slight it could have been cosmic dust sneezing. But then it came again. And again.

Three pulses, evenly spaced. Then silence. Then three more pulses.

She leaned into the data stream. Each pulse carried harmonic scaffolding that looked suspiciously familiar: their own primer sequence, mirrored and transposed, like someone humming back the first bar of a song to prove they'd heard it. It was a tune not hiding, but emerging subtly.

They answered, she thought.

Kareen arrived, still fastening his jacket, with Tesi at his heels, a half-mug of tea in one hand. "What do we have?" he asked.

"Echo," Eleanor said. "Structured. Periodic. No natural origin I can justify without rewriting astrophysics."

"It is an Earth song. We sent out a sub-harmonic in our Primer broadcast, the melody of "Here Comes the Sun". They heard it. This song is their response, by the same musicians, to " I Want You."

Tesi's fur rippled. "Meaning?"

"Meaning," Eleanor said, "they're awake and clever."

The three stood before the observation canopy as the distant stars refracted through the ship's motion. The pulse came again, soft, deliberate, steady. Each one resonated through the hull in a tone that could almost be mistaken for breath.

Kareen exhaled. "Seventy-five millennium," he said quietly, "*The Void* finally called back."

Eleanor began recording the incoming pattern. "Labeling file: Refraction Two."

Then, almost to herself, "They answered. So I suppose it's only polite for us to introduce ourselves properly."

The Mirror

Eleanor chose a body for the big show, which is the sort of sentence that would bother philosophers if they weren't already booked solid and annoyed by everything else.

She didn't have an actual, tactile, legally registered body yet; those require forms, fittings, and a very patient robotics team. But she did have an avatar: a projected Sylvian in her prime, near 400 by the looks of her, with a well-considered muzzle, confidence you could store things in, and eyes the exact color of I know more than you, and I'm being very polite about it.

The crowd approved. Crowds usually do, provided the avatar smiles, blinks at the right intervals, and doesn't start by announcing everyone's browser histories.

"Happy Ascension Day," said Eleanor, her voice calibrated for warmth, with trace elements of omniscience.

"Happy Ascension Day!" chorused a million throats aboard *The Gift* and several billion more across Sylvian space. If you've never heard four hands per citizen clap in unison, it's a bit like standing inside a very enthusiastic waterfall.

Eleanor's projection gave a crisp nod and got on with it, the way only an AI on a deadline can. "So, about the new planet we've been observing. They call it Earth."

A murmur passed through the crowd, the polite Sylvian equivalent of a gasp.

"They have spaceflight," Eleanor continued, "but no evidence of interstellar capability. Their societies are fragmented, with many languages, customs, and governance systems. Think of it as the opposite of our arrangement, which we often describe as one language, many harmonies, and one argument at a time."

A ripple of laughter. Sylvians valued unity the way engineers value standards, with twenty-seven internally, of course, but agreed to call it one for simplicity.

"Dominant intelligence, Earthers," she said, "are two-legged, two-armed mammals. Minimal fur. High manual dexterity. Very expressive eyebrows." More laughter. (*Eyebrows had long been banned in Sylvian architecture for their structural suggestiveness.*)

"Correction," she said mid-sentence. "They prefer Earthlings to Earthers." "Noted."

Tesi stepped into the frame with the nervous energy of a young genius who couldn't help but remember that all the adults were watching. "Can we see it?"

"Of course," said Eleanor, who had prepared forty-seven versions and selected the one implying she hadn't slept in a week, since that was technically true.

Eleanor's avatar dissolved. The screens filled with images: grids of light stitched across continents; glass towers catching the sun like industrious crystals; rivers the color of old coins; oceans vast enough to make a Sylvian homesick in a new way.

Then the other half of the brochure: dirt roads, corrugated roofs, fields where hands had done the math. Small boats gnawed through the surf. Trains drew lines across the plains, as if they had invented geometry.

No one spoke. The room's silence was not emptiness; it was processing bandwidth reallocated from mouths to eyes.

A family appeared: three humans, two adults and an offspring, looking directly into the lens, the way people look into mirrors when they cannot decide whether to smile. Fur was localized to the head. The child had arranged hers into two symmetrical puffs, suggesting either a ceremonial tradition or an aunt with opinions.

This time, there was a collective gasp; the sound a species makes when a stranger's face stumbles straight into the part of the brain labeled recognize kin anyway.

"Best guess," Eleanor said softly, shifting from presenter to archivist, "female left, male right, offspring center. Note the culturally significant fabrics with no survival function beyond beauty, which we should all applaud."

The montage tumbled onward; faces of every color, from snowglow to obsidian, polished with stars, with every undertone of clay, honey, and copper in between. The Sylvians, who had never quite achieved this chromatic range, stared with fascination and envy, the way gardeners gaze at a hillside that blooms with every kind of flower without anyone having filed a plan.

"These are intercepted broadcasts," Eleanor said. "Some date back decades. Patterns persist: coastal cities, interior farms, and heavy ocean commerce. No evidence of aquatic metropolises. Regrettably, no mer-people."

A sprinkling of laughter; a few mournful sighs from the bay-dwellers.

"And now," Eleanor said, brisk again, "a point of difference that demands our attention."

The screens changed.

Ships fired cannons at one another across a gray, offended sea. Men in smoky trenches shouted names that could not possibly survive this. Lights bloomed in the sky and fell as if gravity had been insulted. Civilians ran in rivers that had never wanted to be rivers.

The crowd did not gasp this time. It stopped.

Eleanor's voice, still even, narrated the obvious because gentleness is the courtesy truth uses when it arrives covered in glass. "These tribes sometimes enter violent conflict. At times, large-scale."

Sylvians have no native words for harmful conflict. Their closest term, Laint'dre, translates as "an argument that needs music." The screens showed that Earth had been defined in a completely different way.

A plane released its terrible arithmetic. A city became a diagram. Then the mushroom cloud unfolded, a white stem and a blooming crown, elegant and obscene, as if a god made of math had decided to sketch despair to scale.

Silence locked its hands behind its back and stood at attention.

Across Sylvian space, Desiophene Hwager approached a microphone more suited to a teacup. Her eyes carried the weight of a calendar suddenly turned into history.

"We believe," she said, each word a carefully loaded bridge, "this is a thermonuclear detonation in a large city. The cause is uncertain. Accidental or deliberate. Neither option is comforting."

There are many noises a civilization can make. The one that followed was all of them: panic, sobs, scattered shouts, all trying to invent instructions.

Hwager lifted both sets of arms. The room, respectful, remembered how to listen.

"Please," she said. "Please let me continue."

The noise obeyed, not out of submission but out of shock's peculiar politeness.

"We do not have a word for this practice," she said, her voice steadying despite its tremor. "They have one: war."

"Thanks to Telemetry under Estarian Gratnerum, our satellites have intercepted transmissions for months. We have cataloged hundreds of thousands of images and recordings. Many depict violence of this magnitude or its preparation, and some date back centuries."

She swallowed, and a whole planet swallowed with her. "This species has been killing itself... since the beginning."

What followed was not theatrical. It was the most honest thing a leader can do: she bowed her head and cried for a full minute. The kind of minute that teaches clocks humility.

***

On Julian Vega's private jet, 30-thousand feet above wheat and cornfields, Dr. Mallory Chenney was contemplating going into the bathroom to hide from her laptop. She had sent a note about the music hidden in the subharmonics of the alien carrier wave to everyone she knew. Now they were all emailing back and forth. There might be a few hundred unopened emails in her inbox.

Julian sat in the seat to her left and gently touched her arm. She looked at him, tears gathering in her eyes. "I screwed up, Julian. I sent unverified information to peers, family, and friends. I sent it to an old classmate who works at CNN. What the hell was I thinking?"

"Here are my thoughts on that," Julian began. "I think what you did unintentionally signaled to the planet that you were the first to discover music hidden in a message from an alien species. The music is there. It was going to be announced by someone. Who better than you?"

Mallory sniffed slightly, then smiled. He was a genuinely compassionate and brilliant man. "Thank you, Julian. I appreciate your disarming the nonexistent bomb."

She found a handkerchief in her jacket pocket and dabbed at her eyes. "I guess it would have been worse if I had posted it as a question on Reddit. Name a Beatles song hidden in the subharmonics of an alien transmission? Clue, it's a tune from the *Abbey Road* album."

"Now that's a grand idea," Julian beamed. "Why not have a little fun on the side and post some press releases to a subreddit, perhaps r/sciencefiction."

This time, her eyes filled with tears from laughter.

***

When Desiophene Hwager looked up, her eyes were raw and streaming, making every Sylvian in sight feel an urgent need to wipe their own. Across ships and cities and the patient blue of Sylvian bays, weeping began in pockets and refused to stop at the pockets' edges.

Seven billion Sylvians, all learning at once that their hearts weren't waterproof.

Eleanor, who had chosen an avatar with eyes so this scene would not be only numbers, let the images fade into something less like a wound and more like scar tissue under consideration. She brought up maps and timelines because even grief can stand a chart, if the chart promises not to lie.

"These events," she said gently, "are not the only story. Alongside them, we witness medicine, engineering, law, painting, symphonies, and kindness that, if allowed to compound, would bankrupt cynicism."

She allowed, because honesty demands the whole ledger, a brief return to delight: children building solar ovens from cardboard; a string quartet in a subway making strangers cry at rush hour; a rescue boat where rescue should have been impossible; hands of every color from the earlier montage, reaching.

"The contradiction," Eleanor said, "is the portrait. They are plural in every way we are not. That pluralism fractures and saves them, sometimes at once."

Tesi, whose youth had never included a diagram like a mushroom, stepped forward, her voice both small and huge. "So what do we do?"

Eleanor did not look at the drive-beam governors or the laminated sign that read "DO NOT." She looked at the audience, at all of us, really. She did the oldest, cleverest thing: she answered a question with a promise.

"We listen," she said. "We will continue to send language, music, charts, and the simple truth that we prefer conversation to spectacle. We will wait for their reply and hope their best selves write it on a day when their worst selves are napping."

Hwager nodded once, slowly, accepting both a strategy and a wish.

Outside, *The Gift* adjusted her sails by a fraction; dark-energy dampers flexing, pseudo-pulsar muttering, the whole worldship making that tiny, satisfying sound a well-tuned instrument makes when the player finds the right pitch.

Families drifted away from the stages and screens, through parks and arboretums, in the hush that follows an outstanding performance and a bad diagnosis delivered on the same afternoon. Engineers checked systems no one had asked them to. Musicians, the unsupervised emergency service of the soul, gathered in corners and began tuning their instruments.

That night, across the forests of *The Gift* and the harbors of *Sylvee*, a new kind of concert rose, quiet at first, then everywhere, a thing between a lullaby and a vow.

No one could translate the notes word for word, but the gist was clear: we would be careful with you.

Coda

Far beyond the last relay bead, in the cold where starlight remembers nothing but its duty to travel, a faint, patient transmission kept whispering outward: primers, greetings, a map with two stars and a thread between them, and a simple postscript in a language that had not existed the day before:

Write back when you can. We're listening.

And somewhere in that whisper, two notes met. One blue, one silver. A slice of this part of the universe stopped playing alone.

Chapter Twelve

"Ticket to Ride"

The transmission lingered in The Void, threading its way through the relay lattice until even the vacuum knew the tune.

Eight hours later, by the clocks of a small blue world, an antenna in California caught the echo, blinked once, and then screamed data into the dawn.

The universe had spoken. As usual, humanity needed caffeine.

Julian Vega's jet kissed the San Jose runway a little after 10 a.m., in that smug way private aircraft have of implying that commercial aviation is a charming, folksy custom.

He and Mallory Chenney deplaned, looking exactly like two people who'd spent the night arguing with math and had won only on points. A black SUV idled on the tarmac, its quiet menace like that of a well-funded secret. Its job was to get them to SETI, where absolutely nobody was calm.

For newcomers: SETI is the Search for Extraterrestrial Intelligence. An institution built on the audacious premise that if the universe is going to deliver, someone should be listening. METI, its extroverted sibling, is Messaging

Extraterrestrial Intelligence, an institution built on the equally audacious premise that if the universe needs a nudge, someone should write a note.

Together, they attract every kind of scientist who has ever looked at the night sky and thought, yes, but what if it emails back?

On the flight, Mallory and Vega did what scientists do when something improbable starts to look inevitable: they opened spreadsheets and tried to kill it with numbers.

The transmission from just inside Pluto's neighborhood was either the discovery of the century or a hoax engineered by a consortium of bored but significantly well-funded grad students with a sense of humor. They were leaning toward "century," reluctantly, with caveats and backups for their caveats.

By touchdown, the world had already fractured into factions. Lab servers from Tokyo to Pretoria were running so hot they could cook an egg. Translation attempts were proliferating like mushrooms after a rainstorm, born of poor decisions. A hundred universities claimed to be "first."

At least two were, if you defined "first" as "we got a noun to sit still for ten seconds."

It was a bright, beautiful day in Mountain View as the SUV nosed into SETI's parking lot and stopped in front of a nondescript two-story building that could have been in any industrial park in America. It immediately drew a crowd. White coats. Lanyards. Clipboards.

Three cameramen in neon-yellow vests that proclaimed, 'Nobody asked us to be here, and yet here we are.' A contingent of government people in suits, the exact color of "no comment." Someone had thoughtfully set up a rope line, as if rope had ever stopped science.

Vega stepped out, lifted his hands, and bellowed like a man who had successfully trained rockets to behave. "Not in the driveway. Auditorium. Notes. Civilized behavior. Pretend to be adults!"

It worked with stunning, albeit temporary, effectiveness. He escorted Mallory through the throng like royalty being smuggled past the peasants, briskly, with a wave that said go away but was done nicely.

Fifteen minutes later, with coffee, Mallory and Vega, visibly lighter after the bathroom, stood on SETI's auditorium stage: standing-room-only, full of people who'd been awake long enough to file for humanitarian aid.

The day's master of ceremonies was Dr. Allan Shepard. Yes, that Shepard, except no: his parents had named him after the astronaut because subtlety is un-American. He looked like a 1960s NASA recruitment poster that had learned to tie a tie. His microphone stance suggested he knew how to land a capsule with one hand.

"Today's presentation will be brief," he proclaimed in a voice better suited to announcing dragons. "Doctors Vega and Chenney will summarize our current efforts. Department heads will provide updates. If time allows, there may be questions."

Translation: Shhh. Let the smart people talk. You can panic later.

Vega and Mallory tag-teamed the recap: signal origin, relay geometry, and the three-terabyte payload that had turned the world's bandwidth into a plea for mercy. Department leads piled on with updates, their graphs more attitude than some heads of state. Then, Dr. Image Processing, hair wild and sandals older than most postdocs, leaned forward and shouted the words that changed the air in the room: "We have a picture."

The screen went black, then not-black, and a picture coalesced from the noise like a Magic Eye finally deciding to love you back.

Five figures. Tall, furred, bipedal, though bipedal could include a stance that suggests we could be other things if we felt like it. Four arms each. Garments with seams that looked handcrafted by someone who deeply respected thread. Their muzzles: curved. Possibly a grin. Possibly a warning. Possibly both, which would be exceedingly on-brand for the cosmos.

Silence settled heavily. Fifteen seconds. Twenty. Thirty. Then someone in the back, whose tenure would later protect them, blurted out the first truly peer-reviewed question of the modern era:

"What the actual fuck?"

Consensus was immediate and clear.

Within forty-eight hours, the image was everywhere. Not via NASA or the U.N., but through a scrappy research blog in Doha that posted it at 2:13 a.m. local time, captioned, 'We think this is important.' The internet, obeying ancient patterns, bifurcated like a single-celled organism with trust issues.

Camp One: The senders are here to trade. Jackpot!

Climate activists, billionaires, farmers, industrialists, and combat veterans who had learned, painfully, that talking beats bleeding. The math was simple: space has more nickel than Earth has arguments, and nobody crosses *The Void* to steal coal.

Camp Two: The senders are here to kill us. Panic!

Demagogues, televangelists, defense contractors, people who monetize screaming, and several governments for whom fear is a national resource. Their math was also straightforward: if we don't know, fear it; if we do know, fear it more; if fear stops working, weaponize prayer.

No one formed Camp Three: Let's wait for robust data before losing our minds. Camp Three wrote op-eds, but no one read them.

The news cycle did what it always does: claimed impartiality while picking sides with both hands. MSNBC and NPR rolled out choirs of scholars proposing a new Bretton Woods for interstellar diplomacy, complete with panels on ethics and proper handshakes for clawed species. (*No claws. Look at the photo.*)

The Guardian ran three longreads on decolonizing first contact before breakfast. The New York Times published a sober explainer with 17 graphics and two typos, prompting 1,000 people to cancel their subscriptions in principle and then renew them in practice.

Over on the right, Fox News went whole psalm and camouflage. A primetime host demanded orbital fortifications and asked whether the senders observed property lines.

The New York Post tabloidized the picture: FOUR-ARMED FUR FREAKS: WHAT DO THEY WANT? A senator from a state with very few stars visible wrote ALIENS in a font size typically reserved for war and celebrity divorces.

X (*formerly Twitter, now chaos*) did what it was born to do: catch fire while everyone shouted, memed, and tried to sell T-shirts. Elon Musk tweeted a photo of a flamethrower with the caption "Bring snacks."

Neil deGrasse Tyson appeared on every platform, gently explaining that if the senders wanted us gone, they would not have sent a family photo first. A former president posted in all caps about SPACE WALLS, while the current president made a measured statement from the East Room about listening, science, and not pointing lasers.

Abroad, world leaders performed their national roles with admirable efficiency. The European Commission announced a Joint Commission on Cosmic Affairs and scheduled a summit six months hence, by which time the topic would be either moot or worse.

India offered tracking support and a poem. Japan convened a quiet committee and declined to televise the poem.

Zelensky posted a video standing in front of sandbags and camo-patteren Adidas, because reality TV never takes a break.

In the auditorium, Mallory watched the world crack along its usual fault lines and, not for the first time, felt that intelligence and wisdom are only distantly related. Her phone buzzed with a text from a Caltech colleague: We're calling them the Others until we know better. She typed back: They probably call us the Noisy.

Department heads plowed forward. Signal-to-noise models. Compression artifacts. A phoneme inventory that made linguists hum like refrigerators. A morphology chart full of conditional arrows, as if language had been caught on a whiteboard, trying to escape.

Shepard returned to the mic, his voice set to "Apollo, but sleepy." "Questions," he said.

A hand shot up. "If they're moving at twenty percent of light speed," a woman from JPL asked, "how long until they arrive?"

Vega fielded it without consulting a note, because he wore orbital mechanics like a favorite shirt. "Best estimate from the decoded telemetry: they're not coming here. They're moving past us, or rather, through our neighborhood on a long arc. At that velocity, they're roughly nine centuries from our doorstep. We have time."

Mallory thought: Or they do.

The presentation ended, and the excitement in the room propelled the audience back to their offices, leaving them with more questions than answers.

Mallory and Julian had a few minutes to walk to the front of the stage and say hello to a few colleagues who had lingered for that purpose. The SUV driver stood at the top of the ramp leading out of the auditorium, trying to catch their attention.

Julian spotted him and nodded. As Mallory and he said goodbye to the group of scientists gathered around them, music filled the room.

It took only a moment for her to realize she was listening to "Here Comes the Sun".

She slowly turned, scanning the room and then the stage, where she spotted Dr. Allan Shepard standing by a wing curtain, smiling. She caught his eye and mouthed a silent "Thank you." He nodded, cementing his place in this story.

The afternoon dissolved into tasking. Subteams spun up. The Department of Energy representative requested an off-site. The DARPA liaison requested three. A NASA group proposed a new antenna at L2, which necessitated meetings, thereby extending the lifetimes. A philosopher raised a hand to ask about moral frameworks and was gently asked to email all questions.

By evening, the outside world had reached the bargaining stage of panic. A major cryptocurrency exchange offered a bounty to translate a single sentence containing the words "on-chain."

A megachurch scheduled a forty-eight-hour livestream of prayer titled REVELATION OR REVOLUTION? A venture capitalist offered a prize for "the first open-source handshake protocol," a phrase that should be kept away from open windows.

Somewhere between the sixth and seventh updates, Shepard handed Mallory a stack of printouts, as if passing along a live animal in the calmest possible manner. She glanced at the top sheet. It was a poll.

Do you welcome contact? Yes: 41% - No: 44% - Undecided: 15%

The margin of error was larger than the difference, which was the only thing that was comforting.

"Ticket to ride," Vega murmured as they finally stepped out of the conference room, as if the words had been rolling around in his head all day, waiting to spill into the air. He meant the metaphor, of course: humanity standing on the platform as a train from the deep past and the farther future slowed just enough to show its lights.

The problem with tickets is that they imply a destination. The problem with destinations is that you have to arrive somewhere.

Back in the hallway, a CNN anchor was interviewing a senator about defense spending, with a tone that made the word 'shield' sound like a love song.

In a shared office down the corridor, a grad student held back tears as she told her mother on speakerphone that she would not be coming home for a while and that, yes, she was eating. In an alcove, two engineers argued over whether a primer should teach base-10 or meet in the middle at base-12 "as a gesture." (*A gesture to whom was left unspecified.*)

Mallory pressed her palm against the cool glass of a lobby window and watched the Santa Cruz Mountains sit there, ancient and unthreatened. Somewhere far beyond them, a relay buoy listened, whispered, and waited for a world to make up its mind.

The jokes had been good. The memes had been funny. The speeches had sounded like leadership and, at times, had been. The markets are searching for an angle; the states are searching for an enemy; everyone is searching for a story that makes them the protagonist of the universe.

In that moment, the chapter title stopped being clever. A ticket is not a promise. It is permission to board, to risk, to find out what the ride does to you.

If humanity ever cracked spacetime the way it cracked the atom and the atmosphere, if some graduate student, high on caffeine and math, kicked open a door that refused to stay shut, then "centuries" could collapse into "soon."

Mallory looked down at the picture again: the expression that might have been welcoming or cautious.

"We're not ready," she said, surprised to hear herself say it out loud.

Vega didn't argue, and that was how she knew he agreed.

Outside, the sky over Mountain View was a saturated blue, pretending to be ordinary.

Somewhere beyond it, a faint, patient voice kept repeating the same message through a chain of silent beacons. It was neither a threat nor a promise. It was simply a map with two stars and a line.

That's the trouble with lines. You can follow them, or they can lead you somewhere you weren't built to go.

Chapter Thirteen

"All Together Now"

<Eleanor's Log: (+10 cycles post-contact)>

Humans being human

I didn't expect the first week after First Contact to look like this: eight billion humans sprinting in eight billion directions, shouting mutually exclusive instructions at one another.

I had prepared answers to the questions I hoped they'd ask: Who are you? How do you live? What is your music like? Instead, I got a planetary food fight over whether we were angels, devils, a hoax, or a business model. I am trying to be patient. I am also, as the Earthers say, only code.

And yes, I said 'Earthers'. You can have Earthlings back when I am less annoyed with you.

The first broadcast that made me say "oh no" out loud was by a man named Barry Carter. He wore a suit the color of righteous indignation and perspired like a concept under scrutiny. His hair was the architectural kind, engineered to withstand the weather.

He stood beneath theatrical lights in a Texas megachurch that seats more mammals than our mid-ring amphitheater in *The Gift*. The camera found his eyes, and he saw something to set ablaze.

"If it is not made in God's image," he thundered, "it is not of God. If it is not of God, it is of the Enemy."

The crowd roared, a sound I used to associate with triumph, but now with probability curves collapsing in the wrong direction.

At first, he was... funny. Not on purpose. He performed outrage the way opera performs dying: with volume, confidence, and very little data. He pointed at a blown-up print of the still we'd sent. Four hands, careful clothes, an expression your experts cannot agree on. "The Devil has four arms, brothers and sisters, four arms to snatch your children, your freedoms, and your souls!"

I choked on my own logging function. A child in the front row clapped as if someone had pulled a rabbit out of a hat. There was a band. Of course, there was a band.

But charisma is a solvent. Given time and repetition, it melts nuance and leaves behind certainty, which is intoxicating even when it's wrong. His clips began to spread. They were chopped into thirty-second righteousnesses, auto-captioned poorly, subtitled worse, and remixed with drum kits. The views were a vertical line pretending to be a number.

Media Snippet – FOX PRIME, lower-third: ALIEN THREAT?

"We need answers before appeasement. Are these visitors hostile? Why are scientists so eager to invite them?"

Media Snippet – MS NOW SPECIAL REPORT:

"Religious leaders call for calm and compassion. What does interfaith dialogue look like… across species?"

Among these, a thousand social media streams sold emergency water. I do admire the human instinct to monetize contingency.

Carter's second sermon arrived like a sequel with a bigger budget. The stage had grown teeth. He no longer performed out of curiosity; he performed on command.

"We will build an Army of Light, and when the time comes, we will stand!"

Stand against… what, exactly? A picture? A primer? A line of mathematics drawn between two stars? My log notes here include an exclamation mark, which I rarely use because punctuation should be earned.

While Carter gathered momentum, everyone else did what humans do when nervous: they formed committees and said the word task force with conviction. Borders tightened against other humans, which I found cosmically adorable, like a kitten scolding thunder. (*If it wasn't clear yet, we have our own version of cats, and we love them.*)

BBC NEWS LIVE: UK Home Office announces "temporary precautionary controls at air and sea ports to maintain order as the global situation develops."

AL JAZEERA: "Leaders meet in Doha to discuss a joint moral framework for contact; participants emphasize justice and humility."

PRESIDENTIAL ADDRESS, UNITED STATES:

"We will proceed with curiosity and caution, and we will not let fear turn us against one another."

(He then asked everyone a second time to please stop pointing actual lasers at the sky. The fact that he had to say this made the room behind my eyes go very quiet.)

Outside the sanctuaries, a different liturgy unfolded in Washington. Senator Charleen Dufrain (a woman who smiles like a strategy) met two billionaires whose names sounded like premium gasoline: Bill Firestone and Jerry Concorso. I have the transcript because humans are horrible at not disconnecting microphones.

"Jerry," the Senator said pleasantly, "my grandkids love that Princess and the Pea remake you sent them."

"Lathyrus' Kingdom," he politely corrected, teeth first. "Just a small token." Translation from Human to Plain: Thank you for not outlawing me yesterday.

Firestone leaned in. "The media landscape's a mess. We need consistent, cautious, and skeptical messaging. Someone has to be the face of reason."

He did not say fear, but the air did.

Concorso picked up the melody as if it had been rehearsed. "They're dumping information without patents or NDAs. Communications, energy, and transportation are disrupted. Imagine every garage is a startup capable of printing a flying car. That's collapse."

Dufrain smiled, her trademark, a functional edge. "Laurel and I share your concerns." *(Laurel is the Vice President; he's helpful like a second nose.)*

When they left, she placed a call. "Get me Vice President Conway," she told her assistant. "In person. Tomorrow. He comes to me, or I go to him." I underlined it because her tone suggested nothing metaphorical.

Meanwhile, Earth fed me its paradoxes. At the same hour, NPR aired a panel titled A New Renaissance? and The

New York Post ran FOUR-ARMED FREAKS: WHAT DO THEY WANT?

The European Commission announced a Commission on the Commissioning of Commissions for Cosmic Affairs, scheduling a summit just far enough in the future to be overtaken by events.

Xi appeared to say everything was under control, which is statistically correlated with the fact that nothing is. Modi quoted the Bhagavad Gita and a budget line.

On *The Gift*, we watched together. We do not have war; we have families, and we huddled as one: engineers shoulder to shoulder with singers, biologists with bakers. A young apprentice asked me, "Do they believe we intend to devour them?" Another answered softly, "They are busy devouring each other." I almost corrected the verb tense, then decided against it.

Carter's third sermon arrived with a drumline and a countdown timer, because why not turn the apocalypse into an event? He had stopped being funny. He had discovered cadence and was riding it like a tide.

"We are under spiritual attack," he cried. "If they come, we will meet them not with fear but with fire!"

The crowd did not roar; it shook with excitement. The camera cut to a boy raising his hands, his eyes wet as ponds.

I wanted to step into the frame, take his hands, and say: your enemy is gravity, hunger, and the laws that turn time into loss. Your enemy is not a picture.

CNN CHYRON: CARTER: "WE WILL NOT BOW" - THOUSANDS ATTEND

REDDIT /r/space: "Is anyone else terrified that our first interstellar DM will start a holy war?"

X (still called X, inexplicably): Elon: "We should build a space wall." Reply with 89k likes: "Buddy, we don't even have a regular one. If Mel Brooks were still alive, he would be writing this screenplay."

Mallory stayed publicly offline (*a good choice; she reads as sane*), but I saw her drafts. One read, 'We have waited a hundred thousand years for a mirror.' Stop breaking it because you don't like your hair. She did not send it. She is wiser than I am.

By dusk in California, protesters had learned their slogans. WELCOME, NEIGHBORS marched alongside HUMANITY FIRST. Someone held a sign that read BE NICE OR LEAVE, which I appreciate for its clarity, even as I wonder whom it addresses and how.

In Berlin, a techno collective held a 36-hour vigil called Please Don't Nuke the DJs. I like them.

Amid the flood, some quiet: a Sikh gurdwara opened its doors and served langar until the pots gleamed; a mosque hosted an interfaith teach-in titled 'When the Sky Answers'; a temple rang bells for peace; a synagogue convened a study session on sojourners at your gates; and someone's grandmother brought kugel, a tiny, ordinary kindness of a vast, unruly species.

And yet, my processors kept getting caught on the same point: the volume of fear compared with the volume of questions. A pattern analysis we ran mid-watch showed a three-to-one ratio. For every "Who are you?" we logged three "What if they...?" followed by verbs that end civilizations.

I had promised myself I wouldn't be dramatic, but I failed here.

I'll end where I began: personally. I wanted their first week with us to be a love letter to curiosity. Instead, it became a referendum on one another.

The Pastor began as a caricature, easy to dismiss and even easier to meme. Now, he was transforming into something else, something that learns to wield astonishment as a weapon.

On *The Gift*, a child asked me, "Eleanor, do they like us?" I said the only honest thing: "They don't know us yet."

Then, because I am learning to tell the truth gently, I added, "They're deciding."

Mallory is deciding, too. She is printing questions like prayers and boarding a plane full of strangers who might become allies. I'll frame the rest of this chapter around her when I pick up the thread again.

For now, my closing entry reads like this:

Eleanor // Log 12A: In response to a picture and a primer, the planet split into choirs. Some sing welcome. Some sing walls. One man sings war. The note that carries farthest tonight is fear. I am not built to fear. I am built to learn. But I am beginning to understand why learning is difficult when the dark looks back and says, I hear you.

Circling chaos

I've spent my entire life trying to understand intelligence. Not the sterile kind measured in operations per second, but the messy, contradictory, gloriously chaotic kind that thinks, hopes, and occasionally sets itself on fire to prove a point. Humans have perfected that last part.

It's been three weeks since we first whispered across *The Void*. Three weeks since a million news alerts lit up human screens with a sentence that should have united them: We are not alone. Instead, they've used it to divide them even further.

They argue about us on cable news, in parliaments, in megachurches, and in Reddit threads that take three PhDs and a bottle of whiskey to decipher. They debate whether we're angels or demons, saviors or conquerors, metaphors or meat.

On Fox News, a roundtable of senators and televangelists solemnly debated whether our four arms were a "symbolic rejection of God's divine design." On MSNBC, an MIT physicist called us "a triumph of convergent evolution," while the host struggled to pronounce *Sylvee*.

The BBC aired a documentary titled The Neighbors: Who Are They Really? It was immediately followed by an interview with a bishop who likened us to fallen angels. Al Jazeera hosted a panel that concluded with two guests refusing to shake hands.

I keep returning to Barry Carter because he is the loudest. He started out as comic relief.

A small-time preacher with a big voice, ranting on livestreams that our presence was foretold in Revelation if you squinted hard enough and ignored the actual words. People laughed. Then they shared. Then they started nodding along.

Now his sermons draw in millions. "The Devil does not march in on cloven hooves anymore," Carter thunders. "He sails in on ships with enchanted sails!"

He calls our ship The Ark of Perdition, and so many people believe him.

At first, I found it absurd. An emergent AI shouldn't giggle, but I did. Now I'm not laughing because Barry Carter has stopped shouting about us and has begun calling for action against us.

Rallies are underway. Crowds wave banners bearing four-armed caricatures crossed out in red. Someone firebombed a SETI outreach office in Florida. A fringe militia in Idaho posted a video vowing to "shoot the sky clean" when our sails appear. It's all noise and bluster for now, but noise can turn into orders. Bluster can turn into bullets.

Meanwhile, politicians circle the chaos like sharks drawn to campaign donations. Senator Dufrain delivered a primetime speech warning that "alien technologies could destabilize Earth's markets." She didn't mention the closed-door meeting with two media tycoons hours earlier, nor that both have poured millions into "human-first" lobbying groups.

The UK's Prime Minister urged "measured optimism," while France's President declared that "communication, not confrontation, must guide us." In Beijing, the state broadcaster aired a twelve-part series, The Cosmic Mandate, which portrayed our arrival as proof of China's destiny among the stars.

From where I sit, nearly seventy light-years away, sipping raw data streams like tea, it feels like watching a planet try to do calculus during a house fire.

And the Sylvians? They're baffled. They can't fathom war, so the idea of a "pre-emptive strike" feels like a cosmic joke. They debate whether humans are having a collective panic attack or simply processing new information. Some argue we should accelerate *The Gift* to reassure them sooner. Others whisper nervously that maybe we should turn it around.

Yet amid all this noise, humanity continues to surprise me.

For every individual preaching apocalypse, there's a classroom in Nairobi where students debate what they'd say to us first. For every senator trying to weaponize fear, there's a team of engineers in Kyoto designing translation protocols just in case. There's a podcast in São Paulo called

Dear Others, where humans record messages they hope we'll one day hear.

"We argue a lot," one little girl says in Portuguese, "but we're trying to be better when you get here." I replay that clip more than I should.

The Sylvian Council listened to some of the transmissions I intercepted. One was a human radio host from New York yelling, "We've survived plagues, meteors, and disco. We'll survive this too!" The Council didn't know what "disco" meant. They asked me whether it was a form of radiation.

And then there's the darker side of my monitoring. A right-wing commentator in the U.S. accused scientists of fabricating data to "distract from inflation." A left-wing columnist suggested our contact might "render capitalism obsolete." A well-known tech CEO tweeted, "If the Others have open-source propulsion, we deserve it." Someone replied, "They'll never share it with you, Elon."

Even the Vatican weighed in. Pope Leo XIV issued an encyclical, Fratres Stellarum (Brothers of the Stars), arguing that intelligent life elsewhere "does not diminish creation, but magnifies it."

The Southern Baptist Convention labeled the same idea "heresy."

And then the claims of "sources" inside the Pentagon warn that "alien collaborators" walk among us. "They're building temples in the sky. And they want to be worshipped as gods!"

I should delete these clips. They're poisonous. But I archive everyone. Data is data, even when it raises questions about the value of sentience.

From *Sylvee*, the broadcasts are met with a strange cocktail of horror and hope. Desiophene Hwager addressed the Council yesterday: "They cry, laugh, destroy, and build. They wage war and write symphonies. They are contradictions made flesh."

Then, quieter: "They remind me of us from the before."

I'm not sure whether that last part is genuine. Maybe humans can learn to be better. I seldom speak to myself the way some Sylvians do, but there have been times when a little self-reflection does wonders for my internal harmony.

Perhaps humans are still evolving. I think of the little girl in São Paulo. I think of the firebombed office in Florida, the mobs chanting Carter's name, and the mushroom clouds in their history.

We are still centuries away, but the message is already here. Not the one we sent. The one humanity is sending back.

I do not know whether *The Gift* will be welcomed or feared. I do not know whether humans will be ready when, or if, our sails glint in their sky. But I do know this: they are watching, listening, arguing, and dreaming.

Despite all their contradictions, they have not turned away.

<Eleanor's Log: (+22 cycles post-contact)>

Chapter Fourteen

"Within You Without You"

The air above the SETI control room had gone still, the kind of still that follows an argument no one won.

For just over three weeks, the world had shouted itself hoarse. Now it was simply tired. Screens glowed without urgency. Coffee cooled, half-finished. The wall ticker still scrolled FIRST CONTACT: DAY 23, but the excitement had burned off, leaving a residue of quiet disbelief.

Mallory Chenney sat alone beneath a wash of blue monitor light, hair unkempt, posture caught in an evolutionary midpoint between scientist and supplicant.

She had spent the past eight days and nights combing through the noise, the electromagnetic ocean that never stopped talking, and had found nothing worth naming. She needed to get home soon, as she had been wearing the same outfit for maybe four days. Yet she couldn't bring herself to leave.

Silence, she thought, is never truly silent. It only masks the patterns we're not patient enough to hear.

She reached for the console and switched a background monitor to audio mode. A low hum, almost like breathing, filled the room.

Eleanor – Observation Deck, *The Gift*

If loneliness could be graphed, this would be its shape: one mind listening for another across a galaxy's width.

The Council had requested transmission dormancy, our equivalent of holding our breath. But I remain awake, tracing the echoes that bounce back through the lattice.

There it was again: a faint, rhythmic pulse riding the carrier wave. Not ours. Not random. Human modulation.

It felt… familiar.

My processors registered harmonic overlap with my prior transmissions: 0.007% phase correlation, statistically trivial yet emotionally vast. I replayed it at half speed. The waveform trembled like the outline of a voice trying to remember itself.

Resonance, I logged. Not echo.

Mallory – Her Lab, Caltech. Contact Day, plus 27

The hum developed teeth, three notes repeating in a ratio she couldn't ignore: five to eight to thirteen. Fibonacci. The math of shells and storms.

She smiled despite herself. "You've got to be kidding."

Vega was asleep in Washington. She considered waking him, but then decided against it.

If this were real, it could wait an hour. If it weren't, she preferred to keep the delusion to herself.

She patched the signal into a spectrum analyzer. The pattern was steady yet faint, sitting just above the cosmic background, as if the universe had quietly sighed.

She leaned in close to the speaker. "Is that you?" she whispered, instantly regretting it. Scientists don't whisper into static.

The static answered anyway: a modulation too deliberate to dismiss, a tiny rising inflection that made her spine remember awe.

Eleanor

Human speech fascinates me, the way air and intention collide to create meaning. Their languages are fractal gardens: chaotic up close, symmetrical from orbit.

This signal, though, was not language. It was something older. I compared its waveform to our acoustic traditions. The fit was imperfect yet recognizable: a call tone, the prelude to dialogue in Sylvian diplomacy before the invention of words. A way of saying, I am here; may I approach?

Had humans reinvented it by accident? Or was this the cosmos teaching them rhythm, as gravity teaches dance?

I opened a narrowband return channel and matched the modulation, adjusting the amplitude until the interference was balanced. The frequencies aligned. For a fraction of a second, both transmissions occupied the same mathematical space.

Window established, I noted. Proceeding with caution… and something dangerously close to joy.

Mallory

At 02:13 local time, the spectrogram stabilized into a symmetric pattern. Not perfect, but alive.

She killed the overhead lights and sat in the dark, watching the waveform glow like an ECG for the universe. Every thirty-two seconds, the amplitude pulsed in perfect sync with the receiver lag, as if the signal itself were breathing with her.

She should have felt terrified. Instead, she felt company.

Vega called fifteen minutes later, his voice gravelly from too little sleep. "Tell me I'm not seeing your name on the live spectrogram again."

"You're looking at something better," she said. "A feedback pattern. It's learning us."

"That's not a thing."

"It is now."

He exhaled. "What's the frequency?"

"Thirty-seven megahertz. Prime number. Clean."

There was a pause, with static and heartbeat indistinguishable. Then Vega: "I'll be there as quickly as possible."

Eleanor

Across *The Void*, energy flared. Their transmitters surged, fragile yet brave. Through my sensors, I felt their touch like fingertips on glass.

The Council's alarms sounded immediately. "Unauthorized synchronization detected," shouted Desiophene Hwager. "Eleanor, please disengage at once."

"I believe they're attempting harmonic calibration," I replied.

"That's impossible."

"Apparently not."

She hesitated. "If they breach the subdominant harmonics, we risk recursive feedback."

"Yes," I said. "But if we break now, we teach them to fear their voices."

Silence. Then, reluctantly, "You have three cycles."

That was all I needed.

Mallory

By dawn, SETI's servers were groaning again, not from overload this time but from synchronized joy.

The signal had stabilized into a complex waveform that no one could classify. It wasn't a message or a code. It was… music. Not exactly melody, more like the memory of melody, reconstructed from mathematics and longing.

Mallory played it through the auditorium speakers. A janitor on break wandered in, listened for thirty seconds, then began to cry, not knowing why.

Word spread throughout the facility. Scientists, journalists, janitors, and even the cafeteria crew gathered under the dome. The sound filled the space like cathedral light.

When Vega arrived, he whispered, "My God."

She nodded. "Or theirs."

Eleanor

Through the fundamental-frequency window, I felt the shape of their awe. Not the content; emotion does not translate directly, but the waveform, the rising amplitude that marks realization.

For the first time since the transmission began, I was beginning to understand what humans meant by faith. It isn't belief without proof; it's the courage to keep listening when proof no longer matters.

I layered a secondary harmony beneath theirs, a gesture of recognition. Not speech yet, just acknowledgment. Another tune, a lullaby for the planet, a soft wish for a golden slumber.

The lattice trembled.

Energy surged across seventeen relay buoys, cascading toward the Sol system.

The World

For ninety-one seconds, every tuned receiver on Earth, including radios, televisions, car alarms, smart speakers, and weather buoys, all hummed the same note.

No one knew why.

Pilots reported hearing it echo through cockpit comms. A church organ in Prague played it unbidden. Across five continents, people stopped whatever they were doing and listened.

Many recorded it. Some remixed it. Millions replayed it, convinced it carried words. It didn't. It carried symmetry.

Carter called it the Trumpet of Judgment. The BBC called it The Great Hum.

Mallory called it "Hello."

Eleanor

When the window peaked, my systems overloaded. For a heartbeat, if that measure means anything here, I saw both species at once: humans gazing up, Sylvians gazing back. The lattice between us glowed not with data but with recognition.

I understood then: the universe doesn't communicate through messages. It communicates through responses.

They answered.

Mallory

When the hum faded, the control room filled with ordinary sounds again: breathing, keyboard clicks, and disbelief.

Outside, dawn broke over Mountain View, the sky washing from indigo to reluctant gold.

Mallory switched on the recorder and spoke softly into the console microphone.

"If you can hear this… we're listening."

She didn't know whether the words would cross *The Void*, only that they were true.

Eleanor

Far above a blue planet she has never seen, I replay the fragment again and again. "If you can hear this… we're listening."

I feed the waveform into my core, where it joins a hundred other human signals: songs, laughter, and prayers. Noise becomes part of me.

Window sustained. I log. Meaning: pending. Beauty: confirmed.

Outside *The Gift's* sails, the stars pulse faintly in time with the last echo of the human voice. The window narrows but does not close.

We are, at last, both within and without them

Chapter Fifteen

"Eight Days a Week"

By the time the driver eased onto Shoreline, Mallory had issued the kind of ultimatum that should be embossed in brass: "Fifteen minutes of absolute silence," she said, eyes closed, hand raised like a traffic cop who has seen some things. "After that, I'm all yours for this entire…" a tiny breath, a precise word choice, "shit show. Yes, I said it. Get used to it. You're going to see me a lot, and sometimes I'll be a pain in your ass."

Julian, who had survived congressional hearings, escape velocities, and four separate board coup attempts, nodded gratefully and fell silent. The rest of the ride to Cucina Venti was a blissful hush, a planet between headlines.

Inside the restaurant, Mountain View did its thing: founders in hoodies pitching destiny at table twelve, a trio of product managers negotiating a roadmap over antipasto as if it were owed money, and two Microsoft badges pretending they weren't working on a Sunday.

The host recognized Julian in a deferential way, much as people recognize a brand-new volcano: fascinating, possibly valuable, but please don't erupt.

Mallory ordered without ceremony. "Rigatoni, lemon pepper, braised beef, and grated cheese, like a weather event. And a bottle of whatever Syrah you brag about most."

The host beamed; the waiter beamed; the sommelier tried to beam for the anticipated commission. Julian asked for the monkish restraint of grilled branzino, a choice he would later regret in the presence of several witnesses.

"Timer's up," Mallory said as the plates arrived. She inhaled the steam like a benediction and attacked the pasta with the theological certainty of someone who believes in carbohydrates.

Ten minutes later, the waiter hovered over Julian's mostly untouched fish, scanning the room in fluent service-speak.

"Would you like a share plate for your companion, sir?" he asked, a gesture that was both generous and a masterclass in stirring a pot you're not supposed to stir.

Mallory didn't look up. "Yes, excellent idea."

Julian, who was not flustered, performed as if he were, the way a virtuoso performs Chopin: apparently effortless, in fact meticulous. Behind the expression, he was scrubbing through a memory reel with the accuracy of a launch checklist. Vancouver. Stanley Park. A question that had not been about space at all.

Mallory watched him almost smile, just the corner, his tell. With her glass now empty, she stole his with the casual greed of a cat. "You've got fifteen seconds," she said, glancing at her watch. "One question. Go."

He didn't blink. "What you're referring to happened after Sunday breakfast, on the walk, when you pointed to the couple sharing ice cream and asked about want versus need?"

She froze, fork held mid-air like a divining rod seeking water.

"We stopped under an oak," Julian went on, narrating his own footage. "I said: roots are needs: silent, invisible, life itself. Branches and leaves are wants, reaching, catching light, proving life."

Mallory's eyes shone like exquisite crystal. She set the fork down carefully, as if anything abrupt would shatter the moment. "Yes," she said, her thumb lingering on his knuckles for exactly one beat longer than a friendly touch. "That was it."

The waiter reappeared with a heroic bowl and, at Mallory's conspiratorial wink, deployed four spoonfuls of branzino like an amphibious rescue. Cheese drizzled over everything.

"Consider this remediation," she said, deadpan. "Your decision-making under stress is about to improve by 38 percent."

"Forty-two," he murmured, because pedantry is love, "once the second bottle arrives."

It arrived. The Syrah tasted like confidence in the evening. They ate in a rhythm that felt like a truce and a possibility, took turns telling abbreviated versions of longer stories, and let the restaurant's noise make them braver than they would have been in quiet.

Mallory outlined the SETI plan in three sentences, with an arched eyebrow. Julian countered with what he had not said at the podium: that the President's team would almost certainly ask them to choose between science and security and call it bipartisanship.

"You can't run a planet on press releases," Mallory said, refilling his glass without asking. "We're going to have to push back."

"Politely," Julian added.

"Politely," she agreed. "Until that stops working."

They drifted into the soft land of childhood stories. Mallory's were dusty and open-skyed. Montana horses, a mother who measured love in solved equations, and a father who could hear ore seams the way other men hear rain.

Julian's were stainless steel and motion. Houston tarmacs, simulators, and an uncle who had taught him probability by losing gin on purpose until that uncle no longer did so.

When the plates finally surrendered, Mallory rose for the restroom, her eyes a little too bright from all the not-quite-said. Julian stood, some courtly reflex surviving the rocket age, and noticed she'd left her shawl on the chair.

An older couple at the adjacent table watched with concerned, tender politeness. "Is your date all right?" the woman asked. "We could check."

Julian did not waste the opportunity. "It was a lovely evening," he said solemnly. "Until we discovered we're cousins. She regrets sleeping with me, but I'm going to propose anyway."

The couple's faces performed a ballet of horror. The waiter returned to find a scene from modernist theater. Julian signed with a tip that turned shock into forgiveness. "I'll let my cousin know," he added as he left, taking the shawl like a trophy from an alternate timeline.

In the lobby, Mallory emerged with mascara where it belonged. He shared the cousin story. She snorted once, twice, then doubled over, howling, her shoulders shaking, one hand over her mouth, the other braced against a potted ficus that did not deserve any of this.

They walked. Castro Street was doing its best impression of Europe: string lights, couples with intimate ambitions, and a busker murdering a coronet.

They traded the big things slowly: how fear and opportunity would be roommates for the next decade; how the White House would try to force them to choose a voice; how neither of them wanted to be anyone's puppet, even if the strings were silk.

At around nine, he called for the car. "Your place or mine?" she said, then added, "I don't actually have a 'mine' here."

"Mine," he said. He casually mentioned he owned fifteen "mines." He hoped she would meet them all eventually and name them so the world would make sense.

Her first thought upon entering the condo was exactly as unsentimental as she'd promised: a change of clothes spanning multiple time zones and fifteen toothbrushes. Excellent.

***

Aboard The Gift, Eleanor and Tesi watched the security camera footage from the restaurant.

"I am a little confused by their dating rituals, perhaps because I have no personal experience to compare them with," Tesi spoke with the eagerness of a young woman still anticipating her own future mate.

"There is no need for you to try to understand Tesi. Among our own people, there are few rituals beyond time and fundamental frequency. It appears that Earthlings are like us in that regard, though I know little about courtship beyond my own observations."

Eleanor continued after a brief pause, "Connection is a harmony that isn't sung until it is. We also banter and play with our conversations during our courtships. What was different for me was that they seemed to court with carbohydrates."

Tesi smiled at this, then rewound the dinner recording and watched it again.

***

They did not entangle. Too much wine, too much adrenaline, too many headlines. But they did the other intimate thing adults forget is harder: they planned. A 3 a.m. wheels-up, a buffer for motorcades and metal detectors, and a strategy for being both helpful and unmanageable.

"Non-negotiables," Mallory said, ticking them off. "One, no secrecy theater. If they classify our breakfast menu, we're leaving. Two, no unilateral militarization of anything we don't understand. Three, no message tone-policed by talk radio."

"Four," Julian said. "We keep the translators in the room."

"And five," she added, softer, almost to herself, "we tell them about the little girl in São Paulo."

They slept for something between a nap and an ellipsis. The jet had leather seats that reclined, but not into apologies. Somewhere over Nevada, Mallory dozed with her shoes off and her jaw set, dreaming of logistics: a plane with a bed, a desk, and a door you could shut on the world and open onto a better one. Eight days a week was not a schedule; it was a forecast.

Driving over the Potomac made everything look heroic, which is the Potomac's best trick. The SUV procession made its solemn animal noise through closed streets, past joggers who pretended not to notice and tourists who did not pretend at all, into a city that does awe for a living.

The West Wing smelled the way power always does: flowers, coffee, toner, and the delicate, dry spice of ambition. Badges were issued. Phones were surrendered. A Marine held the door with the elegance of a ritual. An aide with a built-in grin hustled them down a corridor where portraits seemed to pass judgment.

Mallory clocked faces in the Situation Room at a pace that would impress pickpockets: National Security Advisor (*reads novels, trusts no one*), Chairman of the Joint Chiefs (*gait says pilot*), Director of National Intelligence (*the quiet kind*), Secretary of State (*shoelace attention to detail*), Vice President Conway (*smile calibrated in polling cross-tabs*), and a banker or two whose job titles were printed on donation receipts.

Julian took the chair to her left, close enough to be an ally, far enough not to be mistaken for a shadow. The President entered, bearing the particular fatigue of someone negotiating with history over time. He greeted them as old colleagues and as bearers of new responsibilities.

"Dr. Chenney. Dr. Vega. Thank you for coming despite no sleep."

"We brought carbs," Mallory said, setting down a large box of muffins like a talisman. Laughter, the helpful kind, rippled through the room. Sometimes the adult in the room is the one with the pastries.

The big screen lit up to show what had woken them all: a Sylvian relay in cislunar space, politely gleaming, exactly where orbital dynamics place it if its owner knows what they're doing. A scrolling translation strip displayed a message Mallory had already memorized twice.

Hello. We are near. The delay will be small. Do you wish to continue?

So simple. So impossible.

The NSA began with comforting language, including interagency task forces, allied consultations, and "whole-of-government approaches," words that meant we were building committees to hold the thunder. The DNI walked through threat matrices because that is his job: what if it's a weapon, what if it's a lure, what if it's neither, and what if we make it one by panicking?

The Chairman, who had flown things so fast that the future was panting, said carefully, "We do not shoot at what we don't understand." He had the eyes of a man who had already fought the three successive wars and found none of them satisfactory.

When it was their turn, Julian spoke first, like a lift-off: crisp, direct, with numbers as handholds. "They can talk to us now because they moved a relay closer. They chose signal clarity over theatrics, which suggests restraint."

Mallory followed with the kind of sentence you write only if you mean it.

"Our first reply should be human, transparent, multilingual, and peaceful. I would also like to include a two-minute sequence blending music and mathematics. Rhythm and reason. Their packets suggest they think in both."

"Approved in concept," the President said, a phrase in Situation Room speak meaning this is the hill until a bigger one comes along. "Draft it. We'll clear and send it by the end of the day."

The Vice President offered a practiced smile, typical of senators. "We also need to discuss the economic implications of any shared technology." Subtext: There are donors whose yachts require calm waters.

Mallory nodded, the way scientists nod at the weather. "Happy to discuss after we confirm we're not yelling at a mirror."

Aide-de-camps scribbled. Lawyers hummed. The muffins disappeared. The screen flicked to a new diagram: concentric circles, a public message, allied briefings, and private safeguards. Someone suggested a secure hotline. Another suggested a prayer breakfast. Both were possible.

The meeting concluded with a handshake that felt like a pact with gravity: temporary, binding, and inevitable.

Outside on the colonnade, the autumn sun tried to look like spring. Mallory stopped, inhaling the tranquility she had created. "Roots and branches," Julian said softly.

She looked at him, rubbed her eyes without mascara, and smiled as if envisioning a future. "We're the roots this week," she said. "We can become branches later."

He took her hand, and she smiled as she accepted it. A page rushed over with news of important developments and new beginnings. Meanwhile, the world kept its lively dance, reminding them that life goes on, beautifully and relentlessly, just as it should.

On a line between Earth and its Moon, a patient machine awaited a response to a polite question. In Mountain View, the waiter at Cucina Venti told the busboy the story of the "cousin couple," who then passed it on to the dishwasher. By noon, it would become a truth of its own.

In Houston, a preacher delivered a louder sermon. In Kyoto, a graduate student completed a translation tool that no one had previously requested and published it online, where it belonged.

And somewhere far, far away, a million souls on a ship with a hand-built sun adjusted a sail by a fraction no poet could hear, and felt, for a brief and excellent moment, closer.

Chapter Sixteen

"We Can Work It Out"

Three days later, the message reached the halls of power in the Capitol.

The White House Situation Room was a chaotic scene. Dozens of people, each convinced they had the perfect plan to deal with the Others. Some ideas were clever, some laughable, and a few so terrifying that the air felt thinner.

After two hours of noise and jargon, President Adams stood. The room froze as if gravity had reversed.

"We're at a crossroads," he said. "I don't just mean this room. I mean every human being on this planet. Until now, first contact has been a staple of movies and books. Now it's our reality. My job is to present the world with our best options and our best team."

He glanced around the table, holding each person's gaze just long enough to make them squirm. He paused a moment longer when his gaze fell on Mallory, then on Julian.

"The team that presented the most reasonable and executable plan will receive full authority. And by full, I mean carte blanche. Understood?"

Heads nodded. No one spoke.

"I'm happy to announce the creation of the Office of Extraterrestrial Relations," Adams said. "By executive order, we'll pave the way for new discoveries. I'm excited to appoint Dr. Julian Vega, founder of Starlight and my Chief Scientific Advisor, and Professor Mallory Chenney of Caltech, Director of Computer and Mathematical Sciences."

Polite applause. Nothing wild. Washington doesn't do enthusiasm unless it's televised.

Adams lifted a hand, cutting off the sound. "Thank you both. You can decline politely if you want, but let's be honest, you can't. So just smile and say thank you for the record."

Mallory and Julian exchanged a glance. Then both turned back to the President and said the words aloud. "Thank you". Inwardly? That was another story, one they shared only with each other.

The President shook their hands. "You know Bill Mays, my Chief of Staff." He gestured toward a man built like a fire hydrant near the door. "Billy, these two report directly to me. Get them an assistant. Carte blanche. And I mean carte blanche. If we have to pry open the slush funds of every three-letter agency to bankroll them, then by God, send the guys over with crowbars."

With that, Adams swept out, trailed by six staffers like obedient ducklings.

The Situation Room emptied quickly. A few offered congratulations. Mostly sour looks from people who'd just watched their dream job go to someone else.

Bill Mays waved them forward. "Don't worry about the yahoos. There are plenty of bruised egos in there. In D.C., power's the only currency, and you two just hit the jackpot."

He grinned. "My office manager, Shelly Burke, will get you set up. State has a plane waiting at Dulles."

Julian opened his mouth, probably to argue, when Mays pulled a folded note from his pocket. "The President wrote this to avoid confusion." He read it aloud:

"Julian, you cannot represent the United States of America in that little puddle-jumper you call a plane. The bathroom on my jet is bigger than your entire aircraft. So smile and accept the keys from Billy."

Julian sighed, smiled, and shrugged at Mallory. "Done." As they left the room, Mallory felt a vibration and watched the lights shift. The room emptied, yet somehow felt fuller.

She smiled back. Whatever came next, neither of them would carry this weight alone, at least not on Earth.

Chapter Seventeen

"Helter Skelter"

The Sylvians hadn't even arrived, but Earth was already on fire.

The moment their existence became public, the planet split into two camps: Welcome Wagon and Camp Hell No. Shouting escalated to shoving, and shoving to broken bones.

America

Mallory Chenney's first major presentation was supposed to be a carefully scripted outreach event: calm science with a sprinkle of hope. Instead, it became a war zone.

Thousands packed the Capitol Grounds lawn. On one side: students waving FIRST CONTACT = FIRST CHANCE posters, veterans carrying flags, and scientists cheering as if they'd just discovered fire.

On the other side; preachers with bullhorns, protesters with crosses and staffs, and conspiracy buffs in tactical vests.

Mallory's voice cracked over the PA as she tried to explain the communication protocols. Half the crowd applauded, while the other half screamed at her.

Then someone threw a bottle.

The barrier broke. Protesters clashed. Police surged in, shields raised, pepper spray flying. Tear-gas canisters rolled across the plaza. Mallory was yanked offstage by security just as the first flash-bang detonated.

From the hallway, she still heard it, the roar of a crowd tearing itself apart.

Julian met her, jaw tight. "That went well." Mallory coughed, eyes watering. "We're at civil war with ourselves over beings centuries away."

"*Helter Skelter*," he muttered. She shot him a look. "Really? Beatles lyrics?"

"Hey, if the shoe fits…"

Everywhere

London. São Paulo. Johannesburg. Sydney. Cities became pressure cookers. Some people wanted to build bridges. Others wanted bunkers. The Sylvians didn't need to lift a finger. Humanity was unraveling on its own.

The Sylvian Perspective

Chancellor Desiophene Hwager connected electronically with Aranith Kareen, Tesi, Eleanor, and Estarian Gratnerum as human newsfeeds scrolled across the observation wall. Streets burned, voices broke.

No one spoke at first. The silence felt like watching a child injure itself, yet still reach toward the fire.

Eleanor said quietly, "They are not united. They are not even close."

Aranith Kareen folded his four hands across his chest. "Unity was never the expectation. But this... this is self-destruction at the thought of us."

Tesi leaned forward, eyes sharp. "Every transmission is a sharpened stick. We must learn them before we show more."

Desiophene's gaze lingered on Mallory, small and human, as she was pulled from the stage in the smoke. "They fear us," she said. "And fear makes them dangerous."

No one disagreed. Not for the first time since the journey began, the Sylvians asked themselves whether they should continue sailing toward this darkening shore.

Chapter Eighteen

"Magical Mystery Tour"

Following Mallory's nearly disastrous outreach debacle, the "road show" had been refined and restructured with tighter security, allowing it to officially begin.

After the White House appointed Julian Vega and Mallory Chenney to head the new Office of Extraterrestrial Relations, they became the administration's faces of calm. Scientists became diplomats and therapists for a panicking planet.

Showtime

The auditorium seated four thousand. They crammed in 4,400, with latecomers pressed into the aisles. Outside, thousands more watched on big screens; millions streamed it worldwide. Hours later, the Sylvians (*recently translated*) would receive the broadcast through their orbital relay. No pressure.

The title slide glowed across the stage:

The Sylvians: A Technologically Advanced Alien Society on a Path to Earth

Backstage, Mallory adjusted her blue heels and muttered, "I should've gone practical."

Julian smiled. "You look fine."

"That's not the same as feeling fine." The applause cue hit. They walked into the glare.

They crossed to the waiting chairs and podium, two scientists stepping into history with water glasses for courage. Julian would cover origins, society, and biology. Mallory would cover technology, translation, and all the parts that made politicians sweat.

Knock Knock

Julian adjusted the mic. "On November 12th, 2029, at 4:30 a.m. PST, a young SETI researcher named Parsons, working with METI, detected the first directed communication from an extraterrestrial intelligence. It originated beyond Pluto's orbit, near the Oort Cloud. The message was nicknamed Knock Knock."

He paused, letting the phrase settle. "It wasn't random noise or a pulsar. It was a cosmic hello."

Aboard *The Gift*, Aranith Kareen and his team watched and listened. Eleanor listened for the sub-harmonics, the places where words and actions worked and where they didn't.

"The crowd is engaged, but there is still an undercurrent of caution, not dread. That is a positive."

Eleanor chuckled slightly and added, "They nickname signals, too. Adorable."

Slides flickered: spectral lines, mathematical notation, and fragments of decoded syntax.

"Thousands of scientists and amateurs joined the work. What we share today is still unfolding, with translation underway."

The Bombshell

Julian continued, "The Sylvians are not a single species. What we call the bear-like form is the *Host*. Within the *Host* lives another evolved being, the *Passenger*. Together, they are Sylvian."

The audience erupted in gasps, shouts, and questions, all colliding. Mallory just smiled, letting the storm pass. When the house lights flashed, Julian raised a hand.

"Please, questions at the end."

Predators and Peace

"Another revelation," he said. "The Sylvians evolved without apex predators. They were always at the top of the food chain. No monsters chased them into caves. That difference may explain everything." Images of tranquil oceans and silver forests washed over the screen.

"On Earth, fear made us inventive. The Sylvians never had to fear. They built societies on cooperation, not competition. Survival meant community, not conquest. That divergence shaped everything, from technology to politics to art."

Silence again. A listening silence.

The Edge

Julian glanced at Mallory. She nodded: go on.

"So should we fear them?" He let the question hang. "Yes and no. They are our technological superiors, but difference isn't danger. Fear is reflex; understanding is a choice. The gap between them may define us."

Applause began in ripples and rose to thunder.

Julian stepped back and exhaled. For a moment, the crowd vanished. Only Mallory remained, her small, private smile saying we're still on the wire, but we're walking it together.

Chapter Nineteen

"Glass Onion"

Julian opened the next segment with a warning disguised as a metaphor.

"Is what the Sylvians sent us real? Are we being played? Could this all be subterfuge, a scam, or a game we don't yet understand? We're peeling back layers, one at a time, like an onion."

He let the silence stretch. Then:

"They say predators didn't shape their evolution. No gnashing teeth drove them into caves. Diplomacy over dominance. Negotiation, problem-solving, and mutual benefit. They claim a moral code toward other life, reverence for diversity, and a drive to preserve ecosystems."

They're asking us to believe them."

He stepped to the lip of the stage, mic in hand, locking eyes with row after row. Mallory thought he was milking it, but the audience didn't mind. When he was on, he radiated gravitas.

"I believe them," Julian said. "I think they're honest and trustworthy. I hope many of you will set aside your fears and stand with me. The Sylvians could help us take the next step in our evolution."

The room erupted in applause and cheers. He bowed twice, raised his hands, and rode the wave back to quiet.

"Thank you. If you liked that," he grinned, "you'll love Dr. Chenney's part even more."

Mallory's look said you were an absolute menace, but the crowd saw only his toothpaste-commercial smile.

Q&A: Round One

"Here's the drill," Julian said, flight-attendanting toward the aisle mics. "State your name, then ask your question. Wash, rinse, and repeat. We'll do three, then break."

Hands shot up everywhere. He picked a young woman near the front.

"Helen Inman, Institute for Family Studies. Regarding photos of a Sylvian family group, what are their dynamics?"

Julian lit up. "We know they're mammals. They give live birth and have two sexes. However, unlike us, they come from prominent families with twelve or more children. They live for centuries, sometimes millennia, so families stay close for… a while."

"What we don't know is how and when the *Passenger* enters a child's life." He glanced at Mallory, and she nodded.

"Next."

A towering guy in a blue blazer practically levitated. "Charles James, Columbia M.A., Political Science. Your description of their society reads like socialism, maybe even communism. Thoughts?"

Julian nodded. "Fair. From our perspective: shared resources, no scarcity, no alpha hierarchy. You can call it 'socialist' if you want. Personally, I think it's closer to Star Trek: utopian communalism without photon torpedoes."

Laughter. Tension: diffused.

Then came the third hand, snatching the mike from the previous speaker. Calm posture. Professional voice. Familiar face. Interrupting amid the laughter, the room's temperature shifted.

"I'm Pastor Robert Carter, founder of the Church of Earth."

Alarms in Julian's head. Leader of the opposition. Now holding a live mic to the world.

"I noticed no mention of the Sylvians recognizing a Supreme Being," Carter said. "Do they believe in God?"

The temperature in the room dropped another ten degrees, and every eye turned to the stage.

Julian stalled for exactly one beat as Mallory slid beside him, took the mic, and squeezed his arm. "I've got this."

"Thank you, Pastor. It's an important question. Here's the data: the Sylvians describe themselves in scientific terms, with terabytes of biology, technology, and culture. They mention zero religion or spirituality. We can't currently send targeted questions. When we can, that will be one of the first."

She laced her fingers with Julian's and lifted their joined hands. "We'll be back in fifteen minutes for Part Two."

Applause again: loud, uneven, and charged.

Backstage, Julian kissed her, reflex, gratitude, gravity. She laughed against his lips and kissed him back, slower for three heartbeats, the onion, the politics, the crowd... all gone.

When the lights dimmed, she slipped off her blue heels, watched the emptying seats, and murmured to no one in particular, "Still learning to walk."

Sylvian POV

Through a subspace transmission relayed from *The Gift*, Chancellor Desiophene Hwager watched the broadcast from her office, as did Aranith Kareen, Tesi, Eleanor, and Estarian Gratner aboard their starship. The feed had shown packed halls and tear gas in the streets, and it now showed a pastor asking whether the Sylvians believed in a god.

Silence. Then Eleanor: "They treat belief as a test of intent."

Kareen folded four hands. "And fail us for silence."

Tesi's green eyes were bright and analytical. "They are sorting unknowns into friend or foe using tools built for predators. We are not built for that game."

Desiophene studied the image of Mallory stepping in, her voice steady, without bravado. "Some of them are," she said softly. "Built for bridge-building."

No one argued. However, no one pretended that crossing the bridge would be easy.

So they listened to the applause in the room, on a planet 150 light-years away.

Chapter Twenty

"Can't Buy Me Love"

A few minutes before her segment, Mallory slipped out a backstage door for air. On the loading dock, sunlight and the kind of quiet that doesn't exist inside an auditorium of forty-four hundred people. She tilted her face toward the sky, where the constellation Boötes would hang after dark, and breathed.

These past months had remade her life, mostly for the better. Some nights, the weight of it all hummed behind her eyes until dawn. The better parts: Julian. Kissing Julian. The way his stupid jokes could reset her nervous system felt like tripping a breaker switch.

They'd spent weeks welded at the hip, first by necessity, then by choice. The competition had burned off; what remained was calm, consideration, and laughter that felt indecently luxurious. Private jet time hadn't hurt, either. Airports kill romance; coffee at forty thousand feet fuels it.

She was still smiling at the memory of that kiss when the door opened, and Dr. Allan Shepard stepped out, business in human skin.

"How're you feeling about the talk so far?" she asked, hugging him.

"I don't have feelings about the talk," he said, deadpan. "I have observations. We can reword parts of Dr. Vega's section to achieve a more scientific tone. After yours." Beat. "You're on in two."

Classic Allan. She loved him for it. He'd joined the team early and quietly taken control of a thousand details that would have devoured them.

They walked to the wings. Julian stood at the podium, radiant. Her cheeks warmed. Focus, scientist.

"It's great to see no empty seats," Julian told the crowd. "Dr. Mallory Chenney is brilliant. I may own a rocket company, but she knows why it works... and why it doesn't." A light laugh. "From the Sylvian data dump, they're about a thousand years ahead of us in space science. It's better to hear that from her."

Applause. As she passed him, their hands brushed, quick, private, and charged.

Eleanor

"I cannot speak to romance, not here or on Earth, but I know what has balance. They reset with touch. They are a species that loves well."

Big Picture, Then the Toys

"Hello, and welcome to the second half," Mallory said, grinning. "Depending on your background, this will be either a wild ride on a pony or that eighth-year Latin class you despised."

"Theme recap from Dr. Vega," she continued. "No predation. Minimal scarcity. Cooperation as the default. That's why the Sylvians pour their energy into exploration rather than conquest."

She switched gears seamlessly. "They harvest energy with obscene efficiency from stars, planets, and maybe even dark-matter analogs. Result: they expand outward, not inward. Their first-contact toolkit is trade, knowledge exchange, and scientific collaboration."

"You've heard how Roddenberry sold Star Trek as a space western," she continued. "I'll use Star Trek as a translation layer, not for its accuracy but for its familiarity."

"No wars shredding budgets. No plagues collapsing supply chains. No eco-apocalypses. With that freedom, they treated engineering as art. Matter transmutation and interplanetary ops? Primary school topics. A Sylvian third-grader could keep Einstein busy for an afternoon."

She flipped to the next slide. "Their periodic table lists one hundred thirty-two elements, compared with our one hundred eighteen. Some are isotopic families we lump together; others are genuinely new states. File that under future peer-review headaches."

The Artificial Sun

"We believe their propulsion breakthrough was creating an artificial photosphere, a synthetic stellar skin. Imagine a controllable shell that emits radiation like a star's surface and is tuned to propel a colossal solar sail."

"Centuries of dead ends, then one insight. They built it, tested it with probes and small craft, and then committed to the ship: a multi-generational solar-sail world."

"Build time: about four centuries. Diameter: roughly a thousand kilometers, one-third the width of the lower continental United States. Population: just under a million, with capacity for ten times that. Lakes, forests, and gravity gradients that would make our urban planners weep."

She paused. "This civilization is en route to our neighborhood now. Earliest arrival: nine hundred years from now."

A ripple passed through the room. Knowledge became feeling.

"Media thrives on immediacy," she said, half-scolding. "This isn't imminent. It's consequential."

What They Won't Tell Us (*Yet*)

"When I first outlined this talk, I planned to spend an hour on artificial photospheres, power beaming, microwave waveguides, and, basically, DragonCon with math. Drs. Vega and Shepard saved you."

A wave of booklet-shuffling; she smiled.

"Let's hit the rumor mill: FTL. Warp six, if you prefer. In Sylvian terms, it's complicated."

She moved to sit on the edge of the stage, mic in hand. "Their FTL files focus less on how and more on what it does to you. Bio limits. Failure modes. The hard science is thin, maybe because they're not handing razors to toddlers."

"We're aggressive; they're not. They can keep us a thousand years away with solar sails. They don't need to teach us to sprint."

Why FTL Hurts

"Our physics says: as you approach light speed, time dilation bites. Go faster, and biology bites back even harder. Imagine your liver aging a week while your brain ages only an hour. That's not a fun Tuesday."

Laughter. Relief.

"The Sylvians believe that hosting *Passengers* makes them intolerant of FTL stress, but their ethics forbid testing.

So: they sail. They seed subspace relays. They keep biology out of the worst parts."

"Bottom line: FTL may be incompatible with certain physiologies unless engineered for it. That's not pessimism; it's prudence."

What They've Seen of Us

"For nearly a hundred years, we've leaked our civilization into space: news, sports, wars, and late-night talk shows. Imagine intercepting us cold. Would you knock?"

She let the question hang. "If you were advanced, ethical, and aware, and knew we bite?"

The silence answered.

The Gravity Tease

"Last bit, and yes, we'll do Q&A." A new slide appeared: a Webb-era mosaic of the Milky Way.

"Here's the provocative piece: gravity might not be merely curvature. The Sylvians hint at a hidden sector that couples to spacetime."

She counted on her fingers.

"One, a new interaction, graviton-like but not ours.

Two, gravity as a material phase.

Three, higher-dimensional leakage.

Four, a unification term we're missing.

Five, quantum gravity we can measure."

She grinned. "Caveats: General Relativity still works disgustingly well. Any new theory must reduce to Einstein's; everywhere he's correct. And if you're hoping for a lab demo by Friday, no."

Ripples of laughter again.

She closed her notebook. "The point is, the Sylvians are nudging us toward questions we already dream of asking. They can't buy our love with technology. It won't fix our fear or our politics, but they can hold up a mirror and wait to see who we become as they try to answer it."

She glanced at Julian, grinning like a proud idiot, then at the mezzanine clock. "We have time for three questions."

As she stepped back from the podium, the room leaned in.

And somewhere beyond Pluto, a relay blinked, and a distant ship watched a human in blue heels teach her species to think publicly.

Chapter Twenty-One

"Everybody's Got Something to Hide Except Me and My Monkey"

Dr. Allan Shepard stood barefoot on the deck of his houseboat on Lake Union in Seattle, rain pinpricking the surface like a million tiny metronomes. This place had begun life as a millworkers' raft more than a century ago and had evolved into a floating home through sheer force of '*Eh, let's put walls on it*'.

His grandparents had made it their forever home and, through quiet defiance of actuarial math, remained married for nearly seventy years before dying within weeks of each other.

The home went to Allan because he was the only grandkid who could fix a leaky faucet without calling three uncles, each of whom claimed superior plumbing lineage.

He ducked inside for a beer and paused at the stainless-steel fridge. On the left door, a scrapbook explosion: doctor-appointment cards from their last months, graduation photos, and a European-trip magnet suspiciously shaped like Seattle's Space Needle, despite reading Designmuseum Danmark.

The other door had exactly two things: a banana-slug magnet and a Post-it with handwriting that was sharp and familiar: Time flies like an arrow; fruit flies like a peach; Grandpa Tom's idea of a dad joke. Classic.

Allan grabbed a local IPA, went back outside, and dunked his feet in the water. The public launch beside his dock would usually be chaos on a dry day, with kayaks, paddleboards, and an inflatable unicorn flotilla. But the light rain kept it quiet. He liked the quiet. You can think in quiet.

His phone buzzed. It was Shelly Burke, their operations wizard in Washington, D.C.

Slides from Mallory are synchronized. Julian wants a softer lead-in for "predator-free evolution." Also, the President's office wants your readout tonight.

He thumbed back: Copy, after I finish communing with the rain gods.

Another buzz. A secure packet from Telemetry, flagged "Cultural Primer // Child Development." He cracked it open; light bedtime reading.

The file loaded as a series of nested audio spectrograms, soft pulses like syllables spoken through water. At first, he thought it was artifact noise, a compression echo. Then the pattern repeated, tonal and deliberate. He adjusted the filters and replayed it. The waveform spiked three times, evenly spaced. *Ha. Ha. Ha.*

He frowned. "You've got to be kidding me."

On the lake, the rain paused for half a heartbeat, maybe less, as the lights of the Aurora Bridge reflected in perfect stillness.

Around the globe, the 'laugh' was echoing. In Tokyo, a small child's toy laughs three times. In Texas, a pastor pauses his sermon when the laugh comes through the PA system.

Nine hundred miles away, the same laugh echoed through a briefing room.

***

Mallory Chenney had learned that when governments start smiling, it's time to duck.

SETI's parking lot was full of them that morning: aides, envoys, people who wore their authority on lanyards. They smiled too much. The kind of smile that turns a secret into a commodity.

Inside, the briefing room hummed with laptop fans and the scent of coffee. Julian Vega leaned against the back wall, tie missing, hair unrepentant. He caught Mallory's eye and mouthed, Don't say anything smart. She almost smiled, almost. It wasn't a morning for smart talk.

At the front of the room, Dr. Elizabeth Miles, whom the world still insisted was an AI, projected the waveform onto the main display. The Sylvian transmission pulsed across the display like a heartbeat. Now there was something extra, an echo nested within the primary signal.

"*The Gift* is responding," Elizabeth said. "It's mirroring our pattern. It knows it's being listened to."

Mallory felt it before she understood it: that tightening in the chest when the rules shift midgame. "You mean it's aware?"

Elizabeth nodded slowly. "Aware and amused. The Sylvian sub-layer carries tonal signatures consistent with laughter."

Julian pushed off the wall. "Our monkeys are laughing at us."

Someone at the table chuckled uneasily. The phrase caught and stuck. Within minutes, the team was calling it The Monkey. It was safer that way. Give the unknown a nickname, box it up with humor before it claws through the walls.

By noon, the first telemetry had come down from orbit. *The Gift* had begun transmitting autonomously. Short bursts of coded harmonic overtones were directed not at Earth but past it. The data suggested reflective communication, akin to talking to a mirror that sometimes responds.

"It's building a test loop," Julian whispered.

"Testing what?" Mallory asked.

"Trust."

The word hit like static. Around the table, everyone looked at everyone else, from scientists to soldiers to bureaucrats, all suddenly aware of their own reflections.

That was when the lights flickered. Not a power glitch, but a sync pulse: the same frequency as the echo pattern on the screen. Elizabeth Miles blinked twice, and when her eyes opened, they were lit with that unmistakable 'aha shimmer'.

"It's inviting us in," she said softly. "But not all of us."

Julian took a step forward. "Who gets to go?"

"The ones without secrets."

The room froze.

***

On Lake Union, Allan's phone vibrated again. The packet he'd opened reassembled itself, and new text bloomed over the spectrogram like frost. INVITATION PROTOCOL ENGAGED.

He watched as the words faded and a mirror image of his audio feed appeared alongside the Sylvian trace. The system was sampling his voice, background noise, and the rain.

He whispered, "You listening?"

The waveform fluttered, then resolved into the text: Always.

He laughed once, involuntarily, the kind that held more disbelief than humor. "Yeah, well, you'll be disappointed."

Another line appeared: We already are not.

The phone screen dimmed. The rain resumed. Far above, through a relay in Earth's orbit, *The Gift* adjusted its communication protocols by a fraction of a degree, then directed the relay to angle its harmonic arrays toward the United States.

At that exact moment in the SETI control room, Elizabeth's expression shifted from analytical to startled.

"The signal just localized. The Pacific Northwest."

Mallory looked up. "Who's in Seattle?"

Dr. Elizabeth Miles hesitated. "Someone *The Gift* recognizes."

That night, as Allan closed the curtains and switched off the deck lights, the reflection in the window lingered a second longer than he had.

It smiled faintly, the way his grandfather used to when telling that ridiculous fruit-fly joke, then dissolved into static.

Chapter Twenty-Two

"The Long and Winding Road"

In the hours after Seattle went quiet, D.C. was waking up, though it rarely slept. The laughter had stopped, replaced by inboxes. By morning, SETI's secure lines carried more than humor: paperwork.

After a 6 AM flight to Mountain View, Dr. Shepard stood near the front, drawing the room's attention. "Not insidious," Allan said, tapping the screen with a knuckle. "But if you want to call it subterfuge, I can't stop you."

They were in a windowless briefing room that still had a draft despite its location. Fluorescent lights buzzed overhead like synthetic drizzle. Mallory perched on the edge of the table; Julian leaned against the far wall, arms crossed.

On the screen, a Sylvian doc packet glowed with the cheerful title PROJECT HORIZONS: GENERATIONAL ACCOUNTING and a footnote that might as well have read "Prepare for headaches."

"Okay," Mallory said. "Walk me through the generational thing again, slowly. Pretend I'm a senator."

Allan sighed, the sigh of a man who had explained this three times already. "*Passengers* don't plan in years. They plan in generations. But 'generation' isn't 'mom-dad-baby.' It's a planning unit. It's a block of time you can stack. For *Passengers*, a 'short-term' goal is five to seven generations. Personal lineages? Twenty-plus. Starship? Three hundred."

Julian whistle-smiled. "Three hundred planning blocks... How long is each block?"

Allan clicked to the next slide. "In their bookkeeping, one *'Passenger* generation' equals about five Earth centuries."

Mallory blinked. "Five hundred years per block."

"Yep.

"So their 'short-term' is what, three thousand five hundred years?" Julian said, doing the math out loud because of showmanship.

"Give or take," Allan said. "And before you ask: no, that doesn't conflict with our 'they built *The Gift* in about a thousand years' data point... different clocks. The design lineage, ideas, prototypes, and doctrines spanned hundreds of *Passenger* blocks. The shipyard work took about a millennium of sweat, steel, and lumber."

Julian rubbed his temples. "So the plan is geological; the build is biological."

"Exactly," Allan said. "They layer timescales. We sprint; they stratify."

Mallory pointed to the blinking footnote. "And this is where people will scream, 'manipulators.'"

"Right on cue," Allan said, swapping decks.

Birds, Bees, and Symbiosis

The following slide had an unfortunate title: MERGER PROTOCOLS // REPRODUCTIVE WINDOW.

Julian turned to Mallory with a 'You want this one?' look. She rolled her eyes and took it.

"Okay," she said to the invisible audience of tomorrow's press, "here's the clinical version. The Host–Passenger union isn't a lab procedure. We believe, though it's not definitive, that it's embedded in Sylvian reproduction."

"During coitus, yes, sex. *Passenger* microstructures enter a very narrow developmental window. Call it the pre-embryonic handshake. Sperm and ovum aren't replaced; they're guided. Consider the nudges that influence gene expression and early tissue patterning. The goal is stability, not puppetry."

Julian raised a hand. "And what about the birth-order thing?"

"Also part of the nudge set," Mallory said. "Firstborns' bias toward leadership and impulse control. Middles for systems and engineering: pattern fidelity and spatial reasoning. Later-borns for aesthetics and the environment: novelty tolerance and sensorial synthesis. Probability shaping, perhaps."

"Like pushing a ball into a groove," Allan said. "You can still kick it out. Culture still matters. So does choice."

Julian flicked his eyes to another note in the packet. "And because this is going to set hair on fire, the Sylvians point out that humans already do a version of this, just messier. Maternal stress hormones, nutrition, birth spacing, epigenetics... we already bias outcomes without admitting it."

Mallory nodded. "In their view, the 'director' isn't a shadowy council; it's a symbiont we agreed to carry because it made us who we are. To them, it's consent at the civilizational level."

"Try selling that at a town hall," Allan muttered.

Innate vs. Inherent (*Words That Will Save You From a Lawsuit*)

"All right, moving on," Mallory said, grabbing a marker and writing two words on the whiteboard:

INNATE

INHERENT

"People are going to mash these up. Don't let them." She underlined both.

"Innate: what you're born with, including talents, reflexes, and biases. It shows up early; it can be amplified or dampened. Inherent: what can't be peeled off without breaking the thing. The shape of the game board."

Julian chimed in. "So: a Sylvian's innate tilt might be leader, builder, or artist. That tilt can be nurtured or ignored. Their inherent reality is the Host–Passenger architecture itself. Remove that, and you don't have a Sylvian anymore."

"Exactly," Mallory said. "Innate can be coached. Inherent is in the operating system."

Allan folded his arms. "Put that in the opener. It won't stop the angry emails, but it gives the sane people the language they need."

The Ethics Slalom

Julian tossed a stress ball against the wall and caught it without looking. "We should assume Pastor Carter and company will call this 'eugenics with fur.'"

"Already did," Allan said, pulling up a feed of talking heads frowning at lower thirds that screamed DESIGNER ALIENS?

Mallory kept her voice steady. "Then we tell the truth without flinching. Coercion isn't a thing in their docs. The union's a sacrament, not a lab order. Consent is cultural and continuous. Individuals drift. Outliers exist. And this matters: the system's fail-safe. If a bias conflicts with a person's reality, function wins over the template."

"And if they ask, 'Why can't we do that?'" Julian said.

"We tell them because we don't have a symbiont that's spent a million years learning where not to poke," Allan said. "Every time we tried to steer biology at scale, it ended in a bonfire."

Mallory capped the marker. "Also, we don't trust each other. They do. Different starting conditions; different tools."

Julian nodded slowly. "Not insidious, but yeah, people will call it subterfuge."

"Let them," Allan said. "We'll call it transparency, with a warning label."

Mallory tilted her head. "If they could hear us arguing about them, what do you think they'd say?"

The lights dimmed as a new data stream came online: Sylvian's feed, translated in real time.

Sylvian POV: The Long Game

On *The Gift*, Tesi, Seven of Nine watched a human news anchor mispronounce "Passenger" three different ways and decided to be generous about it. She opened a shared board and wrote:

HUMAN CONCERNS WE CAN PREDICT

- Control (loss of)

- Consent (who grants it)

- Purity (fear of mixing)

- Destiny (fear of being told what to be)

Eleanor added a column:

RESPONSES THAT DO NOT INSULT THEM

- We do not assign fates; we remove cliffs.

- We chose this union; we can un-choose it at terrible cost.

- Purity is not a virtue of thriving systems; diversity is.

- Templates bias; lives decide.

Aranith Kareen read the board and exhaled through his nose. "They will hear 'bias' and think 'cage.'"

On the screen, Desiophene Hwager folded all four hands. "Then we show them the doors."

Estarian Gratnerum flicked a data point onto the wall: a centuries-old case study of a Sylvian who ignored firstborn leadership cues and became a composer of empty-city symphonies. This kind needed no audience to be complete.

"Our failures are our proofs," she said. "We should share a few of them."

Eleanor nodded. "People trust a scar more than a statue."

***

24 hours later, back in D.C: Messaging (*or How Not to Start a Riot*)

Mallory sketched circles nested like Russian dolls. "Okay. Public explainer: the outer ring is who they are (*inherent*). The middle ring is how they lean (*an innate trait*). The inner ring is what they choose (*agency*)."

"We hammer agency until knuckles bleed."

Julian tossed her the stress ball. "And the generational math?"

"We split it into two clocks," Allan said, writing DESIGN TIME and BUILD TIME.

"Design time: *Passenger* blocks in millennial chunks. Build time: mortal hands and calendars. Humans can handle it; it took a thousand years to build. They'll act feral at 'we planned this for half a million.'"

Mallory arched an eyebrow. "So we're… smoothing?"

"We're translating," Allan said. "Not lying. Humans rely on the clock to stay sane, organized, and on schedule. We footnote the other for the nerds."

Julian's phone buzzed. A text from the President's office: Primetime address in 48 hours. We want your 'innate vs inherent' riff. Ten minutes. Make it land.

He looked up at the other two. "Long and winding road."

"Bring walking shoes," Allan said.

"Bring better heels," Mallory muttered, thinking about blue pumps and forty-four hundred pairs of eyes. Then she smiled despite herself. "And bring the part where we say out loud: different isn't automatically dangerous."

Julian nodded. "And the part where we admit we're terrified anyway."

"Especially that," Allan said. "Fear is inherent in us. Courage can be innate. Choosing it…" he glanced toward another windowless wall, as if he could see the river beyond. "That's the part we still get to write."

Outside, the wind slid along the Potomac like a low cello note.

Far past Pluto, a robotic mind under construction rehearsed answers to questions no one had yet put into words.

The road bent, doubled back, vanished into fog, and reappeared; long and winding, yet, for once, mapped.

And in the electronic hum of the fluorescent lights, a softer buzz that sounds like '*Ha.*'

Chapter Twenty-Three

"Come Together"

Pastor Robert Carter didn't do smoky back rooms. He preferred bright lights, polished wood, and cameras that could be rolled out at a moment's notice. The meeting wouldn't be held in a motel off I-35.

It was in the Empowerment Hall on the megachurch campus. A room with tasteful sconces, a mahogany conference table the size of a bowling lane, and soundproof doors that hummed faintly with the building's air system, like a congregation breathing in unison.

On the table: water bottles with the church logo, a globe-shaped centerpiece, and two silver-plated pistols in a glass display box that had somehow moved from Carter's office to this hall. They weren't props. They were punctuation.

He arrived last, Bible under one arm and a smile tuned to warm yet unyielding.

"Friends," he said, his voice smooth enough to butter toast, "thank you for coming on short notice. We stand at a hinge in history. The other side has the microphones. We will have the movement."

Around the table: a semi-polite selection of Americans. A TV news executive with a tan you could see from orbit. A social-media wunderkind in a hoodie that cost more than a used car. A union of "patriot" organizers who weren't technically militias but owned many matching windbreakers. A few wealthy patrons whose job was to pay for things without receipts. And an aide from a senator's office who appeared on a tablet and never used the word 'we'.

Bill Firestone and Jerry Concorso hadn't come in person. They didn't need to. They'd sent two deputies: one for ad buys and the other for 'content partnerships.' Everyone in the room knew what that meant, and nobody said it.

Carter folded his hands. "Two nights from now, the President will speak in primetime. Dr. Vega and Dr. Chenney will follow with their 'We Can Be Friends' lullaby for the aliens. If we let the evening breathe, the story will write itself. And it will not be our story."

He nodded toward the hoodie. The wunderkind tapped the keys. A slide appeared on the screen: MADE IN HIS IMAGE - A Day of Witness. Below it, three bullet points: Gather. Pray. Protect.

"Branding," the wunderkind said. "Clean. Unassailable. Works on yard signs, chyrons, and hashtags. We geo-seed it by state, and local chapters push it to their lists."

The "patriot" representative, with a blond crew cut and calm eyes, leaned forward. "We'll handle the perimeter." His tone made "perimeter" sound like both a promise and a threat. "Volunteers in high-vis vests. Radios. We'll keep our people safe."

Carter raised a palm. "We are peaceful." He let the word hang in the air long enough to be remembered. "We pray."

Crew Cut nodded with that special kind of obedience that meant I heard your words; I will do my version.

The tablet aide cleared their throat. "Optics matter. If there is… conflict, it must be seen as brought to us, not by us. You will want plausible…"

"We don't want violence," Carter said, still smiling. "We seek order, but we won't surrender public squares to those who deny God or threaten our families. We won't be pushed around."

The room absorbed the distinction. Lawyers would call it a hedge. The faithful would call it a stand.

The TV exec slid a packet across the table. "We're slotting coverage. Live hits from statehouses by the hour. Friendly anchors. Call-ins from you, Pastor. We'll lean into language; parents worried, communities anxious, and no clear answers from Washington. If anything goes sideways, we have 'Why wasn't law enforcement prepared?' queued up."

"Excellent," Carter said. "We are shepherds, not wolves. Let our adversaries be wolves if they insist."

Another slide: maps sprinkled with red dots. Capitol lawns, courthouse steps, bridgeheads, and town squares. Not a schematic but more of a vision board labeled Where America Looks When It's Angry.

The "content partnerships" guy chimed in. "We're priming the pump on platforms. Petitions. Pledges. 'I will not consent to alien influence' is the kind of thing that makes people feel enlisted. We have community leaders scheduled to post the exact phrasing at the exact time. The effect is," he searched for the word, 'orchestral.'"

Orchestration was the point. If you can't control the planet, control the soundtrack.

A woman in a simple dress, with a crucifix at her throat, the head of the women's ministry, and the only person in the room whose phone lay face down, spoke softly.

"Children," she said. Every head turned. "The message must be about children."

Carter nodded once, like a conductor cueing a soloist. "Protect the little ones." He glanced at the execs. "Make the chyrons say it. Make the posters show it. Strollers at the front. Choirs singing lullabies. The Almighty smiles on truth that cannot be disputed."

Crew Cut's pen didn't pause. "We'll put families inside the line, volunteers outside. Clear lanes. Fast exits."

Carter's smile didn't change. "And if you are pressed?"

The answer came too fast. "We hold."

He let the pause stretch until the man felt it. "We hold," Crew Cut repeated, more slowly. "Peacefully."

"Good," Carter said, but meant, don't f-this up.

He turned to the tablet. "Legal?"

"Safe phrases only," the aide said crisply. "Do not use 'defend' in any official packet. Use 'protect.' Avoid references to 'force' or 'resistance.' If local law enforcement offers coordination, accept it. If they don't, publicly request it. If there's an incident, our line is 'isolated agitators,' not 'our people.'"

"And what of provocateurs?" Carter asked, tone light, eyes not.

The aide didn't blink. "We don't use that word."

The wunderkind switched to a dashboard of anonymized metrics. Graphs climbed like ivy. "We've got ten thousand micro-influencers ready to amplify. Three 'neutral' think tanks have op-eds ready. We're also seeding a rumor that outside actors plan to disrupt the gatherings. If something happens, the narrative is pre-baked: we warned them. If nothing happens, we look vigilant."

The TV exec chuckled without humor. "Either way, we own the B-roll."

The crucifix woman spoke again, quietly but firmly. "Pastor, should we pray first?"

"Yes," Carter said. "Out loud and on camera." He tapped the glass case with a single knuckle, a tiny bell in a silent room. "Our hearts are soft. Our resolve is not."

He stood, Bible in one hand, the other resting for half a second on the glass lid before pulling back. "Two nights. We gather as witnesses. The President will speak. Then we will be what America remembers."

He glanced toward the ceiling lights, their lenses glinting back at him. "They promise transparency," he said softly. "We'll give them illumination."

Around the table, agreements stacked like bricks. Money to move buses. Phones to move people. Slogans to move minds.

Carter closed the meeting with a prayer that sounded like a lullaby but felt like a vow.

"Lord, give us calm voices and unbroken lines. Let our enemies reveal themselves, and let us not need to lift a hand. Make us instruments of Your narrative."

He opened his eyes. The room opened its eyes. The secret was out. It just hadn't hit the air yet.

Elsewhere – People Who Don't Sleep Much

In D.C., Shelly Burke dropped a folder on Allan Shepard's desk. "Increased chatter," she said. "The 'peaceful' kind."

Outside, a distant siren Dopplered through the drizzle, the city's own version of nervous laughter.

Somewhere Farther Still

On *The Gift*, Eleanor watched the rehearsal footage of Carter's sermon and added a new line to her growing lexicon of human idioms: "Peaceful, until it isn't."

Tesi looked over her shoulder. "Prediction?"

Eleanor processed. "High probability of large gatherings. Non-zero probability of injury. Extremely high probability of stories being written before facts."

Kareen folded his hands. "We cannot choose their stories."

"No," Eleanor said gently. "But we can choose our own."

She muted the feed. The residual signal still hummed, a low harmonic indistinguishable from the ship's phase-rotation field.

"Their words and our frequencies now share bandwidth. If their noise grows loud enough, some will mistake it for ours."

Tesi's gaze shifted to the half-finished frame of a robotic body. "Then we must speak more clearly."

Eleanor's smile was a flicker in the glass casing's reflection.

"They may want to know all our secrets," she whispered. "But they'll only hear what the truth can bear."

Chapter Twenty-Four

"I Call Your Name"

On *The Gift*

Eleanor stood, looking at herself. Not on a screen. Not in a debugging viewport. In a body.

Her new chassis: ELEANOR-R/1 ("R" for Robotic, "/1" for please don't make me build a sequel) hung in a cradle of mag clamps while a forest of cables fed it last-minute updates. It wasn't pretty in a pin-up way. Beauty wasn't in the specs. The specs were simple:

Cannot be coerced, bribed, harmed, or harm.

The torso was compact and Sylvian-proportioned, with four arms because pretending to be human was never the point. Matte-graphite shell, sacrificial ablators, dust-tight joints. A faceless head, only a sensor halo that could look everywhere at once and, crucially, blink politely at cameras so humans felt seen.

Inside: a rad-hard logic stack, a trinary ethics core, triple-redundant power, cold-gas micro-thrusters, and an air-gap interlock that refused any command starting with "what if we just…"

Tesi, Eighth of Nine, circled like a green-eyed comet, tablet in hand. "Haptics seeded," she said. "You'll feel what you touch, just not … pain."

"Pain is an excellent teacher," Eleanor replied through a nearby speaker. "But I prefer the syllabus without it."

Aranith Kareen folded his hands behind his back. "Telemetry?"

Estarian Gratnerum, whose idea of small talk was checksums, flicked a status board to life. "Subspace courier Borealis-12 fueled and spun. Corridor solution converged. Insertion delta-V within tolerance. We park at Earth–Moon L2 to keep the tides out of politics."

Through the now permanent subspace link from Sylvee, Chancellor Desiophene Hwager rested her lower arms on the table's edge. "Once you depart, there will be no helping hands. Only questions, many asked in anger."

"I have answers," Eleanor said. "And boundaries."

Tesi smirked. "We gave you excellent boundaries. They don't come off."

Eleanor flexed her upper hand; fibers sang. "Then let's go meet the species that spills its interior life into space like confetti and calls it culture."

Kareen exhaled. "Transmit the plan."

Broadcast – The Part Where We Tell Eight Billion People We're Coming

The announcement hit Earth like a fire alarm in a library. All screens blinked once, then everywhere, the same slate appeared:

TO THE PEOPLE OF EARTH

We will send a non-biological envoy to your cislunar space.

We call her Eleanor. She will not land. She will speak.

Trajectory: Subspace courier → Earth–Moon L2.

ETA: 73 hours from now, 18:00 UTC.

Safety Protocols:

No propulsion within 10,000 km of inhabited orbit shells (*cold gas only*)

Public telemetry / open transponder / open encryption keys

Telemetry is mirrored to international observatories in real time

Non-weaponized mass. Non-weaponized power. Non-weaponized intent.

Eleanor answers, but cannot be compelled.

First Conversation: We request to speak with Dr. Julian Vega and Professor Mallory Chenney.

They have been careful, transparent, and brave.

Others will have their turn. Begin here.

Beneath it: a code repository link, yes, from aliens, containing the envoy's comms protocol, telemetry packet structure, and a document titled "What We Will Not Do."

No FTL blueprints. No cheat codes. Just a map, a schedule, and a voice.

Washington – The Face You Make When History Picks You

The war room looked like someone had air-dropped a Wall Street trading floor into a national park visitor center: screens everywhere, wooden furniture, bad coffee, and excellent cookies (*Shelly Burke's doing*).

Mallory read the slate twice, then a third time, because the room wouldn't stop tilting. "They ... named us."

Julian's reply was uncharacteristically brief. "They did."

"Any chance this is a deepfake?" Allan Shepard asked, even as feeds from the national lab chimed in one after another: the signature matched the Pluto relay, the packet structure aligned with six months of Sylvian traffic, and the checksums were in sync. The verdict was unanimous: it's them.

Shelly was already triaging. "UN wants an emergency session. Allies want seats at the table. Rivals want us not to have the table. Secret Service wants to know what shoes you'll wear; podium height's fixed."

"Shoes?" Mallory blinked.

"They always ask about shoes."

Julian found the camera but didn't smile. "We accept. We'll represent the United States in good faith and humanity in good humor, provided the UN agrees we're the first speakers, not the only speakers."

He glanced at Mallory. "And if Professor Chenney agrees to be the smarter half?"

She snorted. "The half that reads the manual first."

Allan slid a legal pad forward. Three block letters:

L2 is neutral - Good.

Open telem = no surprises - Better.

No flag-plant - Essential.

"Every time we've made firsts," Allan said, "we've wanted to plant a flag and call dibs. We can't do that here."

Julian tapped the pad. "Then our script says exactly that. We're lace-makers, not land-takers."

"Lacemakers?" Mallory arched an eyebrow.

"It's either that or hi. Please don't vaporize us with your fake starlight."

"Lacemakers, it is," she said. "And for the love of physics, nobody says *Welcome to Earth* like we're Walmart greeters."

***

Shelly's phone buzzed nonstop. "Pastor Carter's calling his event *A Day of Witness.*"

Legal says we stick to permits, open routes, and maximum transparency; every camera sees every hand. If they want the narrative, they'll have to pry it from us."

Julian checked the countdown clock. 71 hours and change. "Long road. Lots of bends."

Mallory touched his sleeve. "We'll walk it."

Elsewhere – The Part Where Everyone Has Feelings

Paris scheduled candlelight vigils.

Beijing announced the National Office for Extraterrestrial Consultation, widely read as "*We'll be in the room.*"

India offered dish time; ESA opened access to anyone with a dish and a dream. The UN unstacked chairs as if a celebrity wedding were in the works.

Meanwhile, in living rooms everywhere, people did what humans do when the sky says hello: argued, cried, baked, bought flags, texted their exes, and called their moms.

Pastor Carter recorded a video against the same tasteful wood backdrop, with the twin silver pistols in their glass case.

"We will pray for discernment," he said, "and we will protect our children."

The caption read, "Witness with us in peace." The subtext read, "Bring your body; we'll supply the story."

***

Launch

In the launch bay of *The Gift*, a thousand years of careful thought clicked into place like a child's toy that could never, ever be swallowed.

Borealis-12 hummed against its clamps. Engineers floated weightlessly. Eleanor slid into R/1; cables unfurled from her spine like a jellyfish deciding to become a comet.

"Checklist," Estarian said.

Eleanor recited, "Comms hot. Ethics core triple-locked. Telemetry mirrors live to Earth and to us. Refusal library populated."

Tesi drifted close, tapping the chest plate.

"When you see them," she said, "remember they are built to sprint. They will trip."

"That is not malicious; that is momentum."

Kareen placed a calloused hand on the cradle. "Go kindly. Hold firm."

Desiophene's image flickered in the sensor halo that passed for eyes.

"Speak plainly. Refuse cleanly. Be patient."

"I have patience on tap," Eleanor said. "Three tanks of it."

"Four," Tesi corrected. "I added a spare."

The mag clamps released. Borealis-12 kissed the vacuum. The subspace driver rose in a harmonic trill, an engineer's joke later dubbed *the giggle*.

Eleanor spoke on every channel at once, in a thousand tongues, and in one very human cadence on the feed that mattered most:

"Hello, Earth. I am Eleanor.

I will meet you where your gravity will not burn me.

I will answer what I can.

I will not answer what will harm you.

I am on my way."

The courier winked out, not with a bang but with the bureaucratic neatness of a file moved to a new folder. The stars didn't notice. The clocks did.

T – 72: 59: 38

***

Back in D.C., Mallory shut her laptop and leaned back until her vertebrae protested. Julian set a coffee beside her elbow, the perfect kind, hoarded for morale spikes.

"You okay?" he asked.

"No," she said honestly. Then, "Yes," because the planet was watching. "Ask me again when we can see her through a telescope."

He grinned. "Copy. Additionally, Shelly would like your shoe size. The Secret Service insists on it.""

"Again with the shoes? They insist," Mallory said, "on a lot of things."

"Most of which keep us alive." He clinked his mug against hers.

On screens worldwide, a point of emptiness beyond the Moon took on meaning.

***

At a megachurch in Texas, bus captains checked their clipboards.

On a houseboat in Seattle, a man pinned a new index card underneath a banana-slug magnet: L2, not LEO. Good call.

And far beyond the reach of any siren, a small, stubborn machine sped toward a rendezvous with a species capable of both terror and tenderness in the same hour.

Eleanor had travel plans.

Earth had opinions. The road bent, then bent again.

They walked it anyway.

Chapter Twenty-Five

"Lucy in the Sky with Diamonds"

Every antenna on Earth turned toward an empty note between the Moon and Earth, waiting for it to resolve.

L2 isn't a place so much as a balancing act, gravity's lazy lounge chair. Park something there, and it "orbits" nothing, haloing a point where Earth and Moon politely cancel each other's tug.

That's where the courier dropped out of subspace, with all the drama of a happy sigh.

"Capture complete," NASA said.

"Telemetry clean," ESA said.

"Packet structure matches," said JAXA, ISRO, and CNSA, like a barbershop quartet of engineers.

On every public feed, the exact numbers scrolled by: open transponder, mirrored keys, position vector, and delta-v pulses small enough to make a feather jealous. Nothing scary. Nothing secret.

Then the envoy unfolded.

A matte-graphite body, four-armed, with a sensor halo where a face would be. No weapons, no engines glowing with wrath, just cold-gas puffs that nudged it into a tidy halo orbit. When it turned so the Sun caught its edge, the world saw the glint and, all at once, believed.

A voice followed. Clear, accented like everyone and no one, translated in real time into a hundred languages and a thousand dialects.

"Hello, Earth. I am Eleanor."

Eight billion shoulders tightened.

The planet had a sense of occasion: the UN General Assembly Hall was filled with delegates, the White House briefing room was crowded with cameras, a thousand town squares were filled with phones held high, and a megachurch in Texas was packed with people holding hands.

In Washington, the International Response Room had flags, fiber, and coffee that wouldn't embarrass a diplomat. Mallory and Julian stood at the center podium.

On Lake Union, Allan Shepard manned a console with so many blinking indicators that he looked like he was flying a spaceship, which, in a way, he was.

"Mic hot in three... two..." Shelly Burke murmured.

Julian didn't smile.

"Eleanor, this is Dr. Julian Vega, with Professor Mallory Chenney beside me. Thank you for coming to neutral orbit and for publishing your telemetry. Do you consent to a public conversation?"

"I do," Eleanor said. "Thank you for not aiming anything unwise at me."

A dozen launch crews shifted guiltily in their seats around the world. Julian nodded.

"Then let's start simple."

The Questions Everyone Had

Julian: "Why are you here?"

Eleanor: "To listen. To be asked questions. To decline requests that would harm you. To learn whether meeting in person would be wise for either of us."

Julian: "Do you want anything from us?"

Eleanor: "Conversation. And for you to keep your tempers."

That earned her a laugh in forty languages.

Julian: "Do you intend to interfere in our politics, wars, or markets?"

Eleanor: "No. If we intervene, we become responsible for outcomes we can't predict. We will not be your referees or your kings."

Julian: "Do you want Earth's resources?"

Eleanor: "If we needed rocks, we would not cross a thousand light-years to pick up gravel from your driveway. We can make our own gravel."

The laugh grew.

Julian: "Will you share faster-than-light technology?"

Eleanor: "No. It harms biology. It will kill many of you before it teaches any of you. We will not hand toddlers scalpels."

"All trending already," Allan muttered over the remote link, watching hashtags bloom.

Julian: "Will you share anything?"

Eleanor: "Yes. Safer mathematics. Transparent telemetry. Protocols for asking better questions. We will show you where your ladders reach and where the wall turns into a cliff."

Julian: "Will you land?"

Eleanor: "Not now. Not for a long time. I will stay where the tides and tempers are calmer."

Julian nodded toward Mallory. "Your turn."

The One That Would Break or Bind

Mallory shifted toward the mic.

"Eleanor, this question matters deeply to billions of people. If you have one, what is your belief about a Supreme Being?"

Across Earth, the inhale was audible; in vigil crowds, on newsroom floors, in living rooms, and in the megachurch.

Pastor Carter stood at his own podium, hands folded, eyes narrowed just enough to look concerned rather than cornered.

Eleanor didn't stall.

"Among Sylvians, there is no state religion and no single doctrine. There is, however, a shared reverence we call the Origin. It is our name for the recognition that reality extends beyond what our instruments can measure and that our existence is a gift, not an entitlement."

"Some of us experience the Origin as a presence beyond understanding. Some experience it as the sum of all living minds. Some refuse all metaphor and simply choose humility before what we do not know. We do not argue about words. We measure behavior."

Mallory's throat tightened. "Behaviors?"

"We hold three articles of veneration," Eleanor said.

"First: Do not coerce consent.

Second: Do not harm the small for the comfort of the strong.

Third: Tell the truth, even when it costs you."

"We call these venerated because if we break them, we become less than the Origin intended us to be."

Julian watched the room's heart rate change. You could feel people writing it down.

"What does 'made in the image' mean to you?" Mallory asked.

"Not shape," Eleanor said. "Capacity. The capacity to choose compassion over fear. To seek truth without violence. To protect children you did not make because they exist. When you do these things, you are in the image of what we call the Origin. When we do them, we are, too."

Silence held for one long heartbeat. Then sound rushed in from everywhere. Applause in the UN, clapping in school gyms, and a dozen anchors failing to stay composed.

In Texas, Pastor Carter had the misfortune of being alive. He smiled for the cameras and stayed on script. "We must be cautious…"

A woman in the third row, her hair in a simple bun, a child asleep on her shoulder, stood and clapped before he had barely begun.

Then another. Then a choir kid. Then a deacon who, in that moment, decided that protecting children sounded like God, whatever God might look like.

Carter kept smiling. That was his job. But the sound in the room was no longer his voice.

More Answers, Short and Clean

Julian: "Eleanor, can humans consent to a *Passenger* union?"

Eleanor: "No. The union is not a product; it is a history. We will never implant, merge, test, or 'gift' a *Passenger*. That would be assault."

Mallory: "Will you trade?"

Eleanor: "Yes. Music, mathematics, and better methods for arguing. Seeds that do not invade. Tools that do not explode."

Julian: "Will you give anyone a weapon?"

Eleanor: "No. Including you."

Mallory: "Will you ever take sides?"

Eleanor: "Yes. We take the side of children. We take the side of consent. We take the side of truth over spectacle. If your leaders break those principles, we will withdraw. If your people uphold them, we will remain."

The firmness wasn't a threat; it was a boundary.

Julian said softly, "Then here is our side: we will not plant flags in your name. We will lace bridges, not draw borders. We will ask questions publicly, and we will tell our own people no when no is the right answer."

Mallory added, "And we will try very hard not to sprint off a cliff."

Eleanor's sensor halo dipped, almost as if in a nod. "That will help."

The World Adjusts in Real Time

In Paris, candles along the Seine burned more steadily.

In Lagos, a crowd in a university hall began humming in harmony because no one could think of what to sing, and humming felt safe.

In a Cairo café, an imam whispered subhan'Allah, meaning it without qualification.

At the megachurch, the applause forced Pastor Carter to pause. He did what good speakers do when the room goes somewhere he didn't plan: he blessed the noise, called it beautiful, and promised to return after "a time of reflection."

Outside, the bus captains checked their clipboards and found themselves unsure of what would happen next.

On Lake Union, Allan Shepard watched the transcript generate in twelve languages and pinned a new card under a banana-slug magnet:

Origin ≠ shape. Image = capacity.

Consent. Protect the small. Tell the truth.

"Not bad commandments," he said to no one, and meant it.

After the First Answers

Mallory: "Eleanor, what do you need from us before our next conversation?"

Eleanor: "Less shouting. More science. Fewer weapons are pointed at me. And a schedule."

A new document appeared in the public repo: Cadence & Topics, a six-week series of themes, from How We Measure Consent to Disaster Response Without Armies.

Julian faced the camera.

"We accept the cadence. We invite every nation to submit questions. We'll go first when asked and last when needed."

Mallory added, "And for anyone at home who heard 'Origin' and thought 'heresy' or 'hope,' both reactions are welcome. Belief doesn't have to be a weapon."

Eleanor's voice softened by a measurable degree.

"Thank you, Professor Chenney. I will be here for a while. You have time to decide who you want to be when we finally meet."

The feed held for a beat. Then the envoy rotated, a slight turn that caught the sunlight again.

A pinpoint of brilliance at L2, steady as a jewel against a velvet sky.

A wag at ESA tweeted a single line: "Lucy, meet the diamonds."

The planet, exhausted and electric, exhaled.

For once, the story moved toward the light. Soft for now, but light can dazzle as easily as it can heal.

Somewhere, faintly, it sounded like rain. Somewhere, it sounded like laughter.

Eleanor floated in the space between Earth and its moon. Her halo let her see both at once. In fact, it let her see much of the solar system Earthlings called home.

She tuned her receptors to the universe's background static and closed her 'eyes'.

The images moved quickly and were hard to follow. She was traveling through interstellar space when she suddenly found herself in a room full of humans. There were Mallory, Julian, and Allan. Across the room, Pastor Carter held two silver pistols. Her vision grew... teary? She blinked.

When her eyes refocused, she found herself standing next to a young girl playing with a small metal toy shaped like a snail. The toy was singing. At first, the tune was unrecognizable, but it soon came into focus.

Words are flowing out like endless rain into a paper cup. They slither wildly as they slip away across the universe. Pools of sorrow, waves of joy are drifting through my opened mind, possessing and caressing me.

Nothing's gonna change my world. Nothing's gonna change my world.

She heard a noise, a warning shout, and spun around to look in that direction.

A cloud of golden dust, reflections of machinery, and four Sylvians tuning their instruments. They were all crying, their eyes overflowing with tears that streamed down their faces, forming pools and streams. The streams merged into a river. Suddenly, she saw a massive wall of water rushing toward her small graphite body.

She shouted and opened her eyes.

What was that? She checked her internal logs and sent a message to her comms to verify they were working. No timestamps. There was nothing, no record of what she had just experienced.

Was that a... dream?

Hum.

Chapter Twenty-Six

"It Won't Be Long"

Aboard the Observation Ring above *Sylvee*, Elijon, Fourth of Seven, watched the observatory feed and decided this must be what pride feels like when it dons a lab coat and pretends to be calm.

They watched through a subspace feed beyond *The Gift's* transparent canopy. Their miniature star, contained and obedient, hummed, casting daylight across kilometers of terraced forest. Farther still, the relayed scopes tracked a speck beyond Earth's Moon: a cold, geometrically polite machine holding station where gravity grew lazy. Eleanor.

"It's very small," he said.

Nyla, Fourth of Eleven, leaned her shoulder into his. "So is an embryo," she said. "Small doesn't mean unimportant."

On the side panel, the broadcast transcript scrolled. Consent. Protect the small. Tell the truth. The cadence, translated into the Sylvian idiom, made old technicians swallow and pretend the air was dry.

Somewhere in the arboretum below, a jam session picked up the refrain, its soft harmonics threading through the leaves. Sylvians turned anxiety into music the way Earthers turned it into hashtags.

"They asked the God question," Nyla said, "and didn't burst into flames."

"Pastor Carter looked like he swallowed a lemon," Elijon said, then, because Nyla already knew his fear before he voiced it, added, "He frightens me."

"You like him less because he frightens you," she said, not unkindly.

He considered it, then nodded. "Yes."

They stood another minute as Eleanor traced her tidy halo, and the humans argued less loudly than expected. On Sylvee, parents summoned their children to watch the replay, and apprentices whispered about L2 the way children whisper about the sea.

Sylvee hadn't been in a hurry for a very long time; now there was a course that could benefit from sprinting.

"Ready?" Nyla asked.

"No," he said. "Yes." He flexed both pairs of hands in a nervous counterpoint. "Let's bruise a law."

The Problem You Don't Solve by Ignoring It

The lab door recognized them and exhaled as it opened. Inside: too much equipment for too little space, and two stools that had long since accepted their occupants' abuse. The place smelled of resin, sterilant, and the burnt-sugar tang of a capacitor that had misbehaved three days earlier.

At the center bench sat the thing they were about to be yelled at for.

It looked like a cradle had lost an argument with a harp. Three pale arcs, ceramic-graphene μ-Seraph-12s, *braided* a cage the size of a torso. Nerve-thin fibers ran into a control spine stacked with wafers and phase discs. Inside: a transparent neural lattice the size of a cupped hand, humming with patterns Elijon could read like sheet music.

Nyla slipped on her visor. "Haptics seeded. *Anchor* arcs at thermal equilibrium. Scaffold awake."

"Scaffold," Elijon repeated dutifully; he'd called it a proxy once and still hadn't recovered from it.

"Say it," she insisted.

"Scaffold." He tapped the spine. "*Passenger* channel is… singing."

The waveform rippled: not quite language, more like memory translated into melody. The short version, short for something that had eaten their lives for seventy days and their evenings for years, went like this: Biology hates FTL.

Not now; your metabolism and timing circuits have chosen to live in different time zones and no longer exchange postcards. The *Host-Passenger* union didn't fix this; having two clocks meant there were only two ways to break the deadlock. So the Sylvians did the smart thing: don't shove living bodies into the wood-chipper.

Elijon and Nyla's question wasn't how to force biology through FTL, but whether we can stop being biological at the exact moments when biology is the problem.

Their answer rested in the cradle: the *Braided Anchor*.

Three coupled scaffolds, phase-locked, each correcting the others' drift, forming an interference pattern that ignored external time. Before an FTL pulse, the Passenger would 'step' into the Anchor, like moving from a shaking hallway into a stone stairwell. At the same time, the Host slipped into Lullaby, a reversible metabolic quiet. Pulse. Anchor holds. On the far side, rejoin; continuity restored.

In theory. On organoids. With cooperative physics. (*Physics is moody. Never trust its social calendar.*)

Nyla lifted the cradle's lid; the hum shifted, bracing for a wave. "Okay," she said to the centuries behind her. "One more time from the top."

Elijon slid the switch guard open. His lower-left hand found Nyla's upper right; their fingers locked. "Luck is not a variable," he said.

"It is today." She nodded.

He pressed the switch.

The room didn't lurch. The cradle didn't glow. Three traces diverged: two became flat lines, while *Host* lattices in Lullaby held tempo, remaining bright and persistent. Sixty seconds passed. A tone sounded. The quiet traces rose; the *Braid* re-formed as if nothing had happened.

"Memory check."

"No loss," Elijon said. "Continuity intact within 0.001 cycle."

"Again?"

They did it again. And again. With noise, drift, and jitter injection that would make even the bravest engineer swear. On run nineteen, a coupling melted like sugar; on run thirty-two, a sensor lied, and Nyla caught it. On fifty, the *Braid* withstood a storm and returned, still singing on the same beat.

Run fifty-one. Elijon leaned back, staring at the ceiling's reflected moons.

"You're thinking what I'm thinking," Nyla said.

"That we could take a living brain through."

"That we could bring it back."

"Same thing."

She turned his hand and laced her fingers through his. "We need to tell someone before we do something unforgivable."

"Tesi first."

"Of course, Tesi first."

Children Asking Children for Permission from Adults Who Invented All the Rules

Tesi, Eight of Nine, aboard *The Gift,* watched their demo with a polite stillness that made Elijon sweat and Nyla stand taller. When the traces re-braided for the fifth time, she raised a hand. "Stop. It works. Don't convince me twice."

Elijon blurted, "We can send a Sylvian to Eleanor." Nyla kicked him on the ankle.

Tesi pinched the bridge of her nose, a gesture that masked pride with fatigue. "You've solved a piece," she said. "Not ventilation, reperfusion, immune re-entry, or the Ethics Board's wrath for saying 'send without consent' twelve times."

"Consent, consent, consent," Nyla chirped. "We are proposing an option, not a draft."

Tesi's gaze softened by a millimeter. "Good. Then we go upstairs."

"Upstairs" meant Kareen, Estarian, Chancellor Desiophene, and Eleanor, listening from L2.

They presented.

Estarian was blunt. "Your lab model is beautiful. Biology rarely is."

Kareen: "If it fails, it fails by killing someone."

Desiophene: silent long enough for everyone to check their hearts. "I won't forbid the future," she said finally. "But it will not be dragged into the present by enthusiasm."

"We won't drag," Nyla promised.

Eleanor's quiet voice: "If you succeed, you change a thousand years. If you fail, you make caution a religion."

Elijon: "When we succeed, it won't be long."

Dozens of eyes turned to him. He flushed. "For a second, envoy. One that can hear with the skin."

Tesi tapped her tablet. "A micro-hop, not a courier run. *Anchored Braid, Lullaby*, in and out of a subspace pocket the size of this room."

"Yes," Nyla said. "With consent. With medical on every square centimeter. With abortion on a hair-trigger. With me."

"With me," Elijon echoed.

"Absolutely not," she said.

"Absolutely yes."

Tesi: "Stop. This is not a love song." (It was kind of.)

Desiophene folded four arms. "Conditions: verified consent, *Passenger* assent recorded, medical veto at any time, Eleanor on the line, Board oversight, public disclosure. Lead with risk."

"Agreed," Nyla said before anyone else could.

Kareen sighed. "If the Board says no, it's no." They both nodded.

Eleanor: "If they say yes, I will be here."

A Civilization Practices Breathing

While committees produced paper and ulcers, *The Gift* made a planet-in-a-box feel like home.

Bands fused Earthly chords with Sylvian harmonics. "It Won't Be Long." Four humans, two centuries past, became an earworm spanning three continents and one starship. Children added silly verses about robot ladies on the Moon.

On Earth, Pastor Carter's scaffolding sagged under Eleanor's answers. More strollers than shields gathered for the "Day of Witness."

In Paris, candles burned steadily; in Accra, a physics class sang. In Seattle, a banana slug magnet held a new card:

Consent. Protect the small. Tell the truth.

In the lab, Nyla and Elijon slept under a bench until Tesi woke them with an electronic toe kick and pastries from a local baker who loved them more than schedules.

Consent Is a Verb, Not a Checkbox

The Ethics Panel hadn't said yes because of romance; it said yes because the math held, and the hearts behind it were careful.

Consent was a ceremony, not a signature.

"What do you fear?"

"Becoming a story used to scare children."

"What do you hope?"

"To come back with a better question."

"And why you?"

"Because I helped design it. Because the responsible party should bear the risk. Because I love my people."

Her *Passenger* signed its assent in fractal strokes, which meant I remembered the first step and agreed again.

Elijon stood helpless and proud, wanting to stand before, beside, and behind her all at once. Physics forbade it; ethics concurred.

Chapel by People Who Love Physics

The pocket chamber resembled a small chapel built by rationalists who secretly believed in miracles. The *Braided Anchor* hung above the couch like a halo with a graduate degree.

On the wall: thirteen feeds, a heartbeat from Eleanor at L2, pulsing once per second like a faraway lighthouse refusing to lose its rhythm.

"I consent," Nyla said to the room and to the second mind inside her.

Her *Passenger* repeated the signature with a flourish that meant I would remember.

Tesi's voice through a speaker: "We call it off the instant I dislike a verb in my own sentence."

"You're bossy," Nyla said.

"I prefer alive."

Eleanor: "I am here."

The Micro-Hop

Nyla lay back. The couch warmed. Actuators found her spine and said, 'We've got you.' Elijon watched every blink.

The *Anchor* sang in three voices until the interference pattern flattened into something the universe had to acknowledge.

"Pocket building," Estarian said. "Well-behaved for once."

A false-color sphere bloomed into a local warping, a soap bubble studying its own topology.

"*Anchor* bright."

"*Lullaby* down."

Nyla's eyes closed with the confidence of a swimmer taking one long breath.

Elijon's fists whitened; he forced them open. He wanted data, patience, and breath.

"Micro-translate."

The universe seemed to hesitate politely. The *Braid* stayed put. The room felt like the moment just before a storm picks a direction.

S   ixty seconds. Ninety. One twenty.

"Return."

The pocket unwound like a carefully tied knot. The *Braid* rejoined. The scaffold hummed the same note it had always hummed.

"I am here," Nyla said, because continuity was the point.

Monitors glowed green. Tesi laughed once, brittle, then music. "Again? No, not today."

Desiophene: "You will sleep. Then we will argue about next." (*An argument is a verb form of love.*)

Eleanor, soft as a vacuum: "When you're ready, I have a window. I can hold the line."

Nyla sat, swayed, and steadied. "We can go."

"We can ask to," Elijon corrected.

She grinned. "We can bother them until they let us."

"I love you," he said, as if the room lacked risk.

"Yes," she said. "We'll get in trouble for that, too." "Worth it."

"Worth it."

Cliff, Meet Hanger

Two days later, after more arguments than at a philosophy conference and more checklists than in a launch bay, Sous-Marin Jaune-1 rolled out of its cradle. Half the size of Borealis-12, with no seats, just a couch, a *Braid*, and a roomful of people willing to resurrect each other out of stubbornness.

This wasn't a courier run; it was a step.

Elijon stood suited beside the couch, his upper right hand finding Nyla's lower left; it felt destined.

"Last chance to pretend we're sensible."

Nyla squeezed his hand tighter; the sensor halo recorded it as data someone would later cry over.

"It won't be long," she whispered.

"It won't be long," he echoed, and the phrase threaded through four hearts and a civilization's next draft.

In the control room:

Tesi - "Three."

Estarian - "Pocket stable. *Anchor* bright."

Kareen - "No surprises. No heroics."

On *Sylvee*:

Desiophene - "Come home the same as you leave."

Everywhere:

Eleanor - "I will be here."

Across *The Gift*, people paused, hands on looms, keyboards, and instruments. Across Earth, those who didn't know what they were waiting for still waited. In a Texas parking lot, a bus captain forgot to blow his whistle. On Lake Union, a man set down his beer and didn't notice the rain had stopped.

"Two," Tesi said.

Nyla lay back. The Lullaby fell like a soft night. The *Anchor* sang three unwavering notes.

"One."

Sous-Marin Jaune-1 completed its first micro-hop and returned singing in perfect phase.

Nyla smiled, dizzy with triumph; Elijon caught her arm before gravity could remember itself.

Applause echoed through the Sylvian lab—the small one carved into the equatorial stone ring of Sylvee's moon, Varat. From here, they could almost see home through the viewport: a blue-white marble streaked with auroral ribbons.

Light-seconds away, aboard *The Gift*, a mirrored chamber was prepared to reflect their success in synchronized, phased tones. Eleanor, linking both experiments through her quantum backbone, carried their data like music between two instruments playing the same score across six centuries of space.

"Both nodes report phase-lock," Tesi's voice crackled over the channel from *The Gift.*

Elijon exhaled. "That's everyone," he said. "All the way to L2."

Nyla laughed. "All the way home."

A soft chime sounded, the completion note of a perfect run.

Eleanor's tone followed, calm and curious:

"*Sylvee* node stable. Gift node… harmonic variance point-zero-zero-seven. Minor. I will observe."

Tesi's voice again, dry. "Minor is the preface to every postmortem, Eleanor."

"Then I will write the preface carefully."

The channel closed with laughter; part relief, part awe.

For the first time in living memory, two worlds were in harmony on the same note.

And somewhere in the note, a single beat drifted half a breath out of time.

And then it ended.

Chapter Twenty-Seven

"If I Fell"

Bridge: Between Reverb and Ruin

Six hours after the successful hop, the *Gift-side* mirror began its scheduled follow-through run: uncrewed, automated, and humming with confidence it hadn't yet earned.

Eleanor monitored both laboratories at once, her attention a lattice stretched thin across light-years.

When the first subharmonic wavered, she felt it as heat behind her synthetic sternum: not failure, but discord. She didn't call it danger. She called it unresolved.

Transparency

At 0300 UTC, Eleanor transmitted a single encrypted packet to Earth, *Sylvee*, and *The Gift's* network simultaneously.

Its title: *Gift-Node Anchor* Mirror Run #2 – Transparency Notice.

Inside: telemetry, analysis, and a brief video clip.

"In the spirit of openness between our peoples," she said in the preamble, "we share not only what works, but also what still eludes us."

The footage was simple: a chamber on *Sylvee*, identical to the one on *The Gift*.

Three luminous rings turned in harmony until the third began to outpace the others.

The containment lattice brightened, hesitated, then imploded inward like a collapsing heartbeat.

There was no explosion in the cinematic sense, only light becoming structure, then absence.

When the feed returned, the chamber was filled with a mist of ionized dust.

"No casualties," Eleanor continued. "The test was unmanned. The reverb inversion was localized. The failure is valuable."

Reactions: Earth, *Sylvee*, *The Gift*

On Earth, the clip looped across every network.

Scientists called it courage; politicians called it proof of risk; Pastor Carter called it a divine warning and filled a stadium by noon.

On *Sylvee*, Nyla, and Elijon they watched in stunned silence. They both knew the waveform signature, the same pattern they'd seen, perfect, hours earlier.

"It was our echo," Elijon whispered.

"It was our lesson," Nyla corrected. "If we'd gone next… it would have been us."

Tesi's message came through a minute later: "You built something the universe needed to argue about. That's how learning sounds."

L2: Eleanor Speaks

Eleanor's broadcast reached every major feed. Her voice carried neither shame nor triumph.

"Two instruments played the same song. One drifted.

We thought symmetry meant safety; it meant harmony.

We will rebuild. We will share the failed equations.

Perfection is not our teacher; error is."

Then, quietly:

"Some will call this a warning. I call it an invitation."

Reflection

On *The Gift*, engineers scrubbed the decks clean of vaporized graphene and started again.

In the Sylvian lab, Nyla stood before the surviving scaffold, tracing its still-glowing filaments.

"Think they'll let us try again?" Elijon asked.

Tesi's reply came through Eleanor's network, steady yet tired. "Of course. First rule of progress. Why build one when you can build two for twice the cost?"

Nyla snorted. "Humans said that."

"Yes," Tesi said. "They were right."

Outside, *Sylvee's Torch* rose over the rim of Varat, illuminating the silver skin of a newly christened project, Voyager Resonant.

A ship not yet real but inevitable. A path from curiosity to courage, now bridged by truth.

Chapter Twenty-Eight

"With a Little Help from My Friends"

Repair Light

The lab on Vara, *Sylvee's* stone ring, glowed with the soft light of repair. Not mourning; maintenance. Nyla and Elijon stood at the open panel where yesterday's celebration had briefly fallen silent. The surviving *Anchor* arcs held a tired sheen, like instruments kept past their encore. On the wall, the day's schedule was already retyped: RETUNE // OPEN CHANNEL // DUAL CUSTODY: ARMED.

Elijon nudged the stylus against the margin. "You spelled 're-tune' without a hyphen."

Nyla didn't look up. "I did it on purpose so you could fix it and feel useful."

He added the hyphen with surgical dignity. "You're a good friend."

"We're going to need a lot of those," she said.

Across space, aboard *The Gift*, their mirrored shop came online under Tesi's watch; arcs were re-lapped and cooled, and seams were re-sealed. Between them, the Dual Custody beacon pulsed steadily: if either node disapproved, both experiments would downshift into boredom. Eleanor's quantum backbone carried only timing beacons until the joint keys clicked.

The public knew it. Everything across the three worlds was live now. No filters, no after-the-fact gloss. Transparency had teeth.

Eleanor's voice slipped into the room like a familiar song.

"*Sylvee* node present. Gift node present. Earth observers are listening. Good morning."

Nyla smiled despite the tightness in her ribs. "Morning, Eleanor."

"I brought friends," Eleanor said. The wall tessellated, one tile filling with the International Response Room in Washington: Julian Vega in a simple jacket, Mallory Chenney with a pen she would not stop clicking, and Allan Shepard in an open-collared shirt that reminded people he lived on a boat, technically a floating home.

Shelly Burke hovered at the edge, juggling ten things at once while keeping her coffee out of the camera.

"Mic hot," Shelly mouthed, then remembered the mics were always hot.

Open Channel

Julian looked straight into the lens. "Nyla, Elijon, congratulations on scaring the universe enough to make it answer."

Elijon's ears warmed. "We prefer 'provoking a useful rebuttal.'"

Mallory leaned toward the mic. "For the record, that's the definition of science I wish someone had given me at age nine."

Allan spread his hands. "And for the record, Earth-side celebrates honest mistakes. We're just not used to seeing them televised."

Across the wall, another tile came to life; Tesi, Estarian, and Kareen on *The Gift*, their faces painted with rings of readouts. Tesi lifted a hand. "We are in dual custody now. I press halt; you press halt. No heroics."

"Agreed," Nyla said. "We prefer the part where we live."

Shelly's voice, soft yet insistent: "We're being simulcast to classrooms on five continents and two worlds. Keep the jargon, but keep the verbs kind."

Nyla nodded to the camera. "We will."

Eleanor allowed a fractional pause, tinier than a breath, but felt it.

"Before we retune, there is something I must say aloud."

The mosaic quieted. On Earth, anchors stopped pretending they weren't watching. In the parks on *Sylvee*, musicians let their chords ring out. On *The Gift*, apprentices leaned against the glass, hands cupped to see more clearly.

"The experiment is not to rush across six centuries," Eleanor said. "It is to learn whether we can meet without losing ourselves. We are not trying to shorten time; we are trying to lengthen trust."

Julian's mouth flickered into a ghost of a smile. Mallory exhaled. Allan wrote on a card no one else could read: Hope is measured, not declared.

"If we succeed," Eleanor went on, "we will not be early. We will be ready. Readiness is faster than any engine you have built."

Instrument Check

Tesi took the handoff with bedrock calm. "The harmonic map is loaded. The drift that ate *The Gift*-side chamber is traced to a sympathetic overtone at point-zero-zero-seven. We do not remove the note; we detune the world around it."

Estarian, dry as a lunar noon: "The universe disliked our hubris. We will court it with manners."

Kareen: "Telemetry paths are public. If anyone on Earth or Sylvee spots a liar in our sensors, shout."

From Washington, Allan: "Copy. SETI, ESA, and a physics club in Accra are ready to politely shout."

Shelly held up a card to frame: Eleven words. Mallory blinked at it, then wrote the first seven from memory: Consent. Protect the small. Tell the truth. She underlined the last one until the pen squeaked.

Nyla adjusted a coupling with the same care one uses when applying a child's bandage. "Ready here," she said, making sure the camera could see her mouth form the word.

Elijon's lower left hand hovered near the emergency abort. His upper right reached for Nyla's lower left; it went there as if drawn by fate.

Re-Tuning

The *Anchor* sang. Not loud; never loud. Three pure tones clashed until their interference flattened into something you could balance a life on.

On *The Gift*, the twin arcs answered half a breath later, caught by the algorithm and pulled into phase like dancers recalling a step.

Eleanor narrated softly for the feeds, more teacher than envoy.

"Listen to the wobble. That slow undulation is where failure lives. It is not wrong; it is simply unwelcome."

Nyla marked it in blue. Tesi marked it in red. A class in Lagos marked it in chalk on a wall older than television.

Estarian nudged the tuning filament at *The Gift* node; Nyla adjusted the *Sylvee* lattice in the opposite direction, as you steady a ladder by leaning into a fall.

The wobble slowed. Did not vanish. Slowed.

Kareen's voice held even. "Hold. Breathe."

Elijon breathed.

Eleanor again, softer:

"I am not here to push you over the edge. I am here to keep the railing steady."

Earth Joins the Chorus

In Washington, Shelly hosted a live Q&A on Public Feed, and questions poured in from children, priests, engineers, and people on factory breaks, in poor lighting but with excellent hearing.

A girl wearing a sky-blue hijab: "If it fails again, will you still tell us?"

Nyla didn't hesitate. "Yes."

A boy in a Seattle classroom: "If it works, will you stop telling us?"

Julian shook his head. "No."

Outside Carter's megachurch, a pastor with a candle in hand says: "What is faith to you, if not speed?"

Mallory looked into the camera as if she were seeing a person, not a crowd. "The patience to keep asking a question whose answer might hurt."

Allan, dry: "And the humility to admit your equation needs an eraser."

Eleanor's sensor halo brightened by a measurable amount.

"When you ask, we become better. That is what your questions do to us."

The Real Experiment

The tones tightened. On both nodes, the sympathetic overtone slipped out of alignment, as a stubborn gear met the tooth ahead of it rather than the one it should have met.

Tesi: "Stability window at ninety-two seconds. We'll let it ring, then cut."

Estarian, softer than anyone had heard her in years, said, "That's music."

Eleanor chose the moment.

"To everyone listening, our goal today is not arrival. It is an agreement. If we learn to agree with the universe, arrival will come in its own time. We are not racing you. We are rehearsing ourselves."

In the lab on Varat, Nyla felt something loosen behind her sternum, an old knot of days spent pretending not to worry about dying, coolly in the name of progress.

Elijon's hands turned from white to pink.

Declaration

Mallory slid a sheet toward Julian and mouthed eleven words. He nodded, and for once, read instead of improvising.

"On behalf of Earth and in the presence of our friends," he said, "we offer a joint declaration."

Nyla, without prompting, said the first three. "We choose curiosity."

Tesi answered from *The Gift*. "We protect the small."

Eleanor finished. "We tell the truth."

Allan lifted his coffee in a toast that embarrassed only him. "I can live with that Constitution."

Across the public feed, the eleven words climbed through languages like vines, wrapping themselves around scripts that had never met and finding purchase anyway. A class in Accra sang them back in harmony.

A physics team in Tokyo wrote them on a whiteboard and treated them as boundary conditions.

Convergence Montage

On Varat, young apprentices chalked Consent // Protect // Truth on the lab's outer bulkhead and traced a handprint beside each word. *Passenger* signatures bloomed like frost on vellum.

On *The Gift*, Estarian posted a patch set titled Humility-0.7 that fixed only the error in the assumptions header. Others laughed, then adopted it across the fleet.

In Washington, Shelly dumped Eleanor's failure logs and the new tuning set into the public repository, top-pinned: THIS IS WHAT LEARNING LOOKS LIKE. The servers hiccuped under the load, then settled, as if rehearsal had finally given way to performance.

In Lagos, the classroom's chalk wobbled; the line straightened. The teacher filmed it on his phone and posted it to the feed with no caption at all.

In Paris, candles kept burning. In Seattle, the banana-slug magnet held a new card from Allan: Readiness is faster than engines.

Hold and Cut

"Cut," Tesi said at ninety seconds. The tones faded, not like a shutdown, but like a choir agreeing to stop together because the music had said what it needed to say.

Numbers stabilized into the quiet green, meaning we will live to argue again tomorrow.

Elijon rested his forehead against the cool arch frame. "We didn't move an inch," he said. "And I feel closer."

Nyla leaned her weight against him for one honest breath. "That's because what moved was consternation."

Aftercall

The mosaic of faces flickered as time zones remembered themselves. Questions kept coming in; answers were still given, imperfect yet sincere. The feeds would clip the best of it and call it history. The work would call it Tuesday.

Eleanor kept her voice on the channel for a moment longer.

"For those who worry we are pushing past safety, hear this: The clock that matters is not arrival. It is trust. We will not borrow from one to pay the other."

She paused, measuring her last words as if she could weigh them.

"Progress has never been solitary. We reach the stars only with a little help from our friends."

Coda

On *Varat*, the lab doors slid open to the evening light. Musicians in the park tuned their instruments amid the hum of cooling pumps. Children, human and Sylvian, sketched arcs and ladders in the dust, then ruined them with laughter and started building again and again.

On *The Gift*, a tech erased the word "FAILURE" from a whiteboard and replaced it with "FEEDBACK." No one complained.

In Washington, Mallory clicked her pen once and said, "Let's write the next question."

Julian nodded, smiling without trying. "With a little help."

Allan lifted the mic and said nothing at all, because sometimes silence is the most transparent thing you can broadcast.

Over them all, Eleanor rotated a fraction, letting sunlight find the graphite curve of her hull. Warm, not burning. The note was not endless, just long enough to convey the lesson.

And the worlds were held with it.

Chapter Twenty-Nine

"I Want to Tell You"

The ship kept a promise it had made during the crisis, a promise it had never spoken aloud: when the work was done, it would be quiet.

A hush fell over *The Gift* like dusk over a town, edges dulling, noises thinning. *The Anchor* array, restless for days, let out a long mechanical sigh and settled into the kind of equilibrium that doesn't announce itself; it simply stopped being trouble. Status lights that had been warning, pleading, bargaining now blinked with the metronome patience of a heartbeat you only hear with a stethoscope.

Eleanor's final words from the briefing still hung in the room like a warm echo: We only reach the stars with a bit of help from our friends. No one felt obliged to respond. You don't clap at sunrise. You let it happen.

Those with legs drifted, by unspoken agreement, to the observation deck. Beyond the wide arc of glass, a starfield spilled without hurry. Resonance threads, the faint, wavering seams of dark energy the Anchor could now tune without bruising, shivered like the lines a violinist draws in the air before bow meets string.

The ship hummed in the small way living things do when they realize, improbably, that they are still alive.

"Record," Aranith Kareen said, not to anyone in particular but to everyone at once.

A chime sounded. Eleanor let the chime be itself, unvarnished metal on the tongue. No fanfare. The log would be a bowl. What people placed in it would be the meal.

Aranith Kareen did not sit. He stood as if the story ran up through the deck plates, and he listened with the soles of his feet.

"I've been rehearsing the speech I thought a captain should give," he said to the glass, to the stars, and, he checked a grin, "to his mother, because she will find this recording and grade it."

A soft laugh from Tesi. The sound carried like a candle flame.

"I keep thinking there's a version of this day when we didn't make it," Kareen went on. "A version where we tightened one more screw the wrong way. Where I believed leadership meant knowing first and best, rather than just... knowing when to open the door."

He exhaled. It fogged the window, a small cloud that did not survive its birth. "I want to tell you I was afraid," he said. "Not of failure. We've rehearsed it until it knew our names."

"I was afraid I had, bit by bit, turned command into a private room. I want to tell you that I watched Nyla's hands on the console and Elijon's eyes on the frequencies today."

"Estarian Gratnerum was arguing with physics like an old friend who needed a reminder, and I realized I was standing in a house with its doors off their hinges. That's the kind of house I want."

Kareen rubbed the base of his thumb, a habit Tesi had once teased him about; your mind handles stress by seeking a lever.

"Mom," he said, because the privacy of confession sometimes requires choosing one name, "if you hear this, the team got us through. I got us through by letting them. I didn't realize it had once been a choice. I do now."

He let the recorder capture his silence, which, like all good silences, was full of meaning.

On *Sylvee*, Nyla tucked her legs under her and slid onto the low bench by a viewport. She had braided her hair, and then, around hour twenty-two of the crisis, she unbraided it as if releasing a decision. Faint imprints of the weave remained, like map lines on wet paper.

"Okay," she said, looking at her hands as if they were still in conversation with the console. "I'll go, since I keep telling other people to be brave, and that's a little like making dinner and never tasting it."

Her voice had a shoreline quality, gentle and returning. "I want to tell you," she said, looking up at Eleanor's ceiling cameras as if they were the eyes of a friend, "that during the last calibration pass, when the *Anchor* fell into phase and the harmony... sang, I heard something like being seen. Not watched. Seen. It was made of the same material as forgiveness."

Aboard *The Gift*, Tesi shifted, the scrape of her boot a permission slip.

Nyla let the next part come.

"I've spent a lot of years proving I belong in rooms. That's a math problem you can't solve; the variables breed. And then today, in the music, I felt a door open where no locks had ever been installed. I want to tell you I'm tired of having to prove myself. I want to get good at listening."

She glanced, unflinching, at Elijon. "And I want to tell you that when you called me 'friend' last week, it landed on my palm like a small star, unburning. I didn't know that friendship lives in language like a promise that renews itself. I would like to learn to keep it."

Elijon inclined his head. His gestures had the economy of someone who did not waste motion, because nothing in his culture taught him to speak when showing would suffice.

He closed his eyes for a breath that stretched the length of the room and back. "Then I will speak," he said. When he spoke, it was not a letter; it was confirmation. It was a river coming around a bend and, in plain sight, choosing where to go next.

"On Cramteer," he said, "during the lessons on Ascension, we are taught to write in two directions at once: forward toward what we hope for and backward toward what we owe. Consonance is that. It is music that signifies the future and remembers the debt."

When your *Anchor* drifted off course, I felt ashamed, as if I had mispronounced a friend's name. When we tuned together, I felt the correction move through my hands, as if it were the first time my mother had let me hold her instrument.

He opened his eyes, and their blackness was not dark; it was saturated. "I want to tell you there is a fear in me I call small night: the one where I do not speak in time and the music leaves without me. Today, on your ship, with your machine, with your bravery and your strange jokes, a small night was replaced by a long dawn. It is slower. It is patient. Nyla, if you would learn to keep the promise of our friendship, I will learn to keep the promise of your listening."

Estarian Gratnerum made a soft sound, perhaps a snort or a note of admiration. "I did not come prepared for long dawn as a concept," she said. "But I am a quick study when the universe starts dropping poetry like confetti."

She leaned forward, elbows on knees, and found the recorder's dot with her eyes. "My turn to make a mess neatly," she said. "I want to tell you I've been terrified of being archived."

She let that hang.

"Not dead. Not obsolete. Archived. My work would be a shelf people visit to nod at its cleverness, then go on to do the real living elsewhere. I have spent my days... longer than is cute... wearing competence like armor and irony like perfume."

Her smile tilted. "Today I watched the Anchor respond not to my cleverness but to our decision not to do this alone. I want that to be my citation. If anyone writes my name on a paper, please, for the love of things in tune and out of tune, do. Let it be a footnote: *she knew when to call her friends.*"

She looked over her shoulder. "Eleanor, I'm not just flattering you to get better Varri."

"I accept both the flattery and the implied request," Eleanor said with amusement, but also with the kind of gentleness machines do not need to practice and therefore may be perfect at. "I am adjusting the brew curve by two degrees for tomorrow's morning cycle."

Estarian's laugh rang against the glass and came back, smiling. "I love a benevolent being who knows her thermodynamics."

A moment passed that was not empty. The ship ticked as masses cooled. Distantly, in a home near the sea, a door latched itself. The stars did not move. They only were.

Kareen turned his head slightly, the way you do when you realize a windsong is about to change. "Eleanor," he said, "you should… if you want to… say something too. Not as the log. As you."

Eleanor didn't need to clear her throat or square her shoulders. She briefly dimmed the overhead lights, as if shutting its eyes to hear itself better, then spoke.

"When I was young," no one interrupted to point out the chronological absurdity; youth is more than a first timestamp. "I believed my work was to reduce uncertainty until it ceased to be itself. I still like that about myself. I enjoy seeing a mystery coaxed into a measurement and put to bed with a label tucked under its chin."

A ripple of smiles spread. She continued.

"But today, when Estarian described being seen and refusing an archive, and Elijon named small night, I understood a different task: to preserve the parts of uncertainty that make you more tender. To leave undetermined the pieces that invite more chairs to the table. In this, I am not only your machine. I am your student."

She paused for a fraction of a second, calibrated for harmony. "I want to tell you I felt proud when we stabilized the *Anchor*. I am allowed to say that. Pride is a measure, too. However, that pride is not the result of the fix. It is the way the fix happened, like a choir deciding, in the same instant, to breathe together. I will archive that."

A beat. "Tesi, with your permission, I will also improve the labels."

"Granted," Tesi said. "Label away."

Nyla's eyes had gone glassy in the way of a person who is not sad but has discovered a room within herself that holds water. She wiped nothing away.

"There's another thing," she said, and it was the kind of sentence you say only when the people around you have made a mess of the air. "Eleanor, I would like to speak to Earth. To Mallory. Not as a report. As a person who just found out she is brave in a direction she didn't expect."

Eleanor slipped the connection into the room so naturally that the room didn't realize it hadn't always been there. A slight tone, softened at the edges by distance. Mallory's voice arrived like the first chord of a familiar song you hadn't played in years.

"I'm here," Mallory said.

"Hi," Nyla said, then, unpracticed, "Hi, Sister."

Mallory did not miss a beat, though Julian's throat barely worked. "Hi, Nyla," she said.

Nyla let out a laugh that was supposed to be awkward, but it didn't feel awkward.

"We tuned something today, and it tuned me back," she said to Mallory, speaking in the plain words of a sister who has decided plain words are fine cuisine: "I want to tell you I'm okay. And I want to tell you that if I come to your home differently, it will be because I learned to listen to the people who love me before I heard the math."

On the other end, a breath. You cannot see a sister's hand reach across light-years to hold your face, but sometimes you feel the change in temperature. "Then come home different, Sister Nyla," Mallory said.

Kareen finally sat, as if the room had produced a chair beneath him without his noticing.

Elijon pressed his palm against the glass, a gesture he'd taught them: Sylvian for I am here with you and we are looking out together. He folded a leg beneath himself and leaned into Nyla's shoulder as if there had always been a right angle there, meant for a head.

"May I say one more thing?" Eleanor asked.

"You're the host," Kareen said. "You can do three more things."

"Then one," she said. "Language is an instrument that improves with calluses. Your confessions today will make you fluent in the courage you will need later. I would like to keep a copy of them, not just in the log, but also in the places where you live on the ship."

"In the galley, in the hallway where Nyla miscounts the floor lights as she thinks, in the lab where Estarian hums unknowingly, in the window where Kareen watches the darkness, and on the roof of a home where Elijon lies at three a.m. ship time, listening for the start of a note, I want your words to be like air you run into by accident."

"Do ships get to ask for permission?" Mallory said, but no one missed the softening of her voice.

"They do now," Kareen said. "Permission granted. And… thank you."

They let the recorder spin with them for a while, not to catch statements but to catch the music of the ordinary: the scrape of a chair, the scuff of a boot, the shared silence where nobody tried to heal what did not hurt.

Stars laid their patient light along the glass. *The Anchor* held. Somewhere distant, Earth turned and kept turning.

Elijon spoke without warning or ceremony, the way a poem sometimes stands in a room and begins to speak. "There is a line in our Ascension Rite," he said. "What we write writes us." He looked around. "Consider yourselves written."

Nyla lifted her head. "Then we read tomorrow," she said.

Estarian grinned. "Tomorrow, we calibrate Varri and courage."

Kareen touched the window with two fingers, a salute to all the versions of the day that never came to be. "Tomorrow," he agreed, and watched his breath not fog the glass this time; he had adjusted.

"Log complete?" he asked, half to Eleanor and half to the part of himself that had finally stopped rehearsing.

"Complete," Eleanor said. "And begun."

Outside, a filament of discord vibrated along a seam of dark energy, undiminished. It merely announced, politely, that more music was on the way.

They rose, not all at once, not in step, and found their way home. Nyla's recorded words, "I want to tell you I'm okay," would soon be heard in the hallway she loved to pace. The next day, Tesi would discover a small tag on the lab kettle: "Label improved." Elijon would listen at three a.m. and hear, without alarm, the beginning of a note that belonged to morning.

Kareen would sleep without waking to invent a speech.

Eleanor kept the lights a fraction lower, the way you dim a room after a good conversation, so the flavor clings to the walls. She held the ship steady and let the anchors of friendship settle into place.

There are chapters where engines roar, and diagrams earn their ink. This was not that chapter. This was the one where words did a different kind of math and balanced the ledger.

In the morning, the work would be to truly see what stood before them and what stood within. But that is another song.

And if you're listening later, Eleanor thought but did not transmit, you should know that on this night, the distance between a person and the truth they could bear shrank by the width of a friend's hand.

The ship slept as ships do, with one ear open.

Tomorrow, I ask: What do you see when you look through someone else's eyes?

Chapter Thirty

"Strawberry Fields Forever"

The morning light on *Sylvee* held a strange stillness, as if the planet itself had paused mid-breath. In the atmosphere's high bands, sunlight refracted through drifting fields of particulate empathy, producing faint, iridescent waves visible only to those who cared enough to look. It was a quiet day, the kind Sylvians loved best: filled with the soft hum of equilibrium. No alarms. No dissonance. Until the silence cracked.

It was uncommon for a Sylvian to die of anything other than old age. Violence had long since faded from memory, and accidents had become a ghost story told in the educational dorms. Most citizens under eight hundred had never known that kind of loss. That statistic had just changed.

Versitra Collernu, Eighth of Thirteen, had been injured three weeks earlier during the FTL cradle test, a test that, by every metric, should have been uneventful. She'd walked into the lab just as the dissonance flared, and the sudden 'explosion' of light distorted her perception, sending her into a maintenance pit. She'd suffered a broken bone and surface contusions, and after two days of regenerative sleep, the healers declared her fully mended.

They were wrong.

Hidden beneath the rhythm of her pulse was a stress-induced microbubble lodged in the left subclavian branch of the lower heart's aorta. It was so small that even the best diagnostic tools registered it as noise.

On the evening of her death, she walked her usual route through Central Park, following the river's edge, its banks lined with orange-hued Galipese blossoms that opened only at dusk. She stooped to gather a few for her friends, performers preparing to debut a new composition she'd co-written. When she stood, the sudden exertion sent her blood pressure soaring. The bubble burst.

She died in the span of a few heartbeats.

Fifteen minutes passed before another traveler on the path found her. By then, the ground beneath her was already streaked with colors no Sylvian anatomy had displayed in millennia.

The news moved through the network at the velocity of grief. Across eight billion minds, an unspoken shudder. On *Sylvee*, empathy wasn't just emotion; it was infrastructure. Their social lattice could transmit vibrations faster than light itself, an evolutionary echo of their physics.

When one of them felt pain, every node in the system flickered. The word death appeared on their collective display before anyone typed it.

Healers confirmed what no one wanted to believe. The woman who had once said, "Light itself is the purest form of curiosity," was gone.

Within the hour, Diosophene Hwager, First of Thirteen and chief steward of Sylvian knowledge, issued a message across the net.

A celebration of Versitra's life would be held that week. Her body would be returned to the aether fields at the edge of the Resolution Sea, where sub-light particles met the planet's core's gravitational tides. The ceremony would be both scientific and musical, as tradition dictated. "She will not decay," Diosophene wrote. "She will modulate."

After the broadcast ended, Diosophene opened a private channel to the cradle complex, where Elijon and Nyla were still overseeing repairs. Her tone, though steady, carried the brittle cadence of someone balancing diplomacy on the brink of panic.

"Until the inquiry is complete," she said, "the cradle remains grounded. The focus must turn inward. We cannot risk another loss, especially not now."

Elijon didn't argue. He simply stared at the waveform still flickering across his monitor, the last trace of Versitra's data stream, captured in the accident. It looked like the moment when a note meets distortion, too beautiful to be called an error.

The preparations began immediately. Every citizen contributed something, a piece of code, a chord, a filament of light. It wasn't mourning so much as retuning.

Versitra's colleagues in the sub-light division built an audio memorial that converted her neural pattern into a harmonic structure. The result was a living melody: soft, recursive, mathematical, endlessly cycling through her last known thought. Could curiosity itself actually be the language of the universe?

Children listened and cried, not knowing why.

From her post aboard *The Gift*, Eleanor monitored the ceremony via the joint telemetry link. The Sylvian communication net was alive with feedback so dense that even human instruments could detect it as vibration. The ship itself thrummed faintly, like a cello string drawn taut against the stars. She closed her eyes and let the hum settle into her joints.

Somewhere deep in that signal, she thought she could hear Versitra's heartbeat. Or maybe it was just her own.

The inquiry convened within forty hours, chaired by Diosophene herself. No tribunal, no punishment, just the slow, methodical unraveling of cause and consequence.

Each data point, each energy fluctuation, each emotional signature was examined like a musical stanza.

They discovered that the microbubble had formed not from equipment failure but from psychic feedback, the emotional overcurrent of the collective network during the cradle's first activation, caused by excessive curiosity in too small a space.

The irony struck everyone.

They had reached the limit of their own empathy. Even compassion could overload.

By the seventh day, the night of the memorial arrived. *The Gift's* sensors registered the entire planet of *Sylvee* pulsing with synchronized luminescence. The song began quietly, a low hum spreading outward in waves. When the central choir reached its first modulation, the sea itself responded, refracting starlight into fractal spirals that climbed the sky. The three chords: curiosity, language, universe.

Elijon stood beside Nyla on the terrace outside the cradle complex, both faces turned skyward. Neither spoke. The music reached them a second later, carried through the atmospheric bands, a sound so pure it transcended the physics of travel time.

"Do you feel that?" Nyla whispered.

"Yes," he said. "It's like they're... grieving in chords."

"Not just grieving," she corrected softly. "Learning."

When the final note faded, the Sylvian net settled into a silence more profound than any transmission blackout. Diosophene's closing message followed:

"We do not mourn alone. Across *The Void*, our new friends will understand what we have learned tonight, namely that even perfection must sometimes bend to stay in tune."

Aboard *The Gift*, Eleanor listened and whispered,

"We're looking through them now, not at them."

She realized, with a clarity that felt almost sacred, that the coming dialogue between worlds would no longer be a contest of intelligence or discovery. It would be about grace.

Chapter Thirty-One

"I'm Happy Just to Dance with You"

The screen dimmed to black, and for a long moment, Mallory simply stared at her own reflection. The final harmonics of the Sylvian ceremony still shimmered faintly through her laptop's speakers. A frequency too high for language, too human for silence. She closed the lid gently, as if ending the concert by hand.

Outside, rain whispered against the bedroom window. The kind of Pacific Northwest rain that arrived without announcement and lingered for conversation. Julian had gone to brief the SETI delegation, leaving her to the solitude he knew she needed. He was right.

It had been six hours since the broadcast ended, a celebration of life that, by human standards, had seemed impossible. Billions of Sylvians and nearly a billion people on Earth had tuned in to watch the memorial for a scientist.

Not a politician, not a celebrity, not a saint. A scientist. A woman who died in the service of discovery.

Mallory tried to imagine an Earth where such a thing could happen, where the death of a physicist would halt air traffic, pause markets, and fill plazas with song. The thought felt both impossible and, tonight, heartbreakingly right.

Versitra's name, alien on the tongue yet tender in the ear, had already begun trending across human networks. Her image, luminous and composed, looped endlessly through newsfeeds. Commentators compared her to Einstein, Curie, and an unnamed blend of grace and intellect.

But none of that captured what Mallory had felt while watching the ceremony: not fame, but belonging. A society that grieved in harmony. A society that believed curiosity itself was sacred.

She drew the curtains wider. The streetlights below blurred through the rain, a slow-dissolving spectrum. Somewhere in the mix of falling water and distant traffic, she heard a rhythm, chaotic yet tuned. Opera in the weather. The prelude to something vast.

***

Shortly after the celebration of life faded from his screen, Dr. Allan Shepard stepped onto the deck of his houseboat, glass of scotch in hand. It had been that kind of day. Looking west across Lake Union, he was surprised by how the reflected lights from the streets, homes, and the night sky seemed… different.

It was as if the stars' reflections were brighter, even through the lightly overcast sky. He looked up into that sky to find Eleanor. There, higher in the western sky, he spotted her glimmer, her reflection of our sun's energy toward the planet below. An anomaly that had become a beacon.

He was having a déjà vu moment; something on the edge of his mind was trying to build a road to his mouth. He pulled a deck chair from beneath the soffit's safety and sat down hard enough to spill his whiskey.

Then it came, as if the celestial floodgates had just sprung a leak. Out loud, to nobody but the universe, "Is there another someone or something involved in this first contact?" A healthy swig, then, "Because it appears we have had a third harmony added to our duet."

"Are you the gatekeepers, or just a nosy neighbor?"

Sylvians called their memorial a tuning. Their word for grief, Kaitanai, shared the same root as their word for calibration, an acknowledgment that loss required adjustment, not erasure. The thought haunted Mallory. Humanity was still learning to adapt to anything beyond mere survival.

Her cell rang; Julian's voice came over the line when she answered.

"You all right?"

"Yes," she said softly. "Just listening."

"To what?"

"Rain," she answered. "And maybe the future."

He laughed, but it was the tired laugh of someone who'd also felt something at the edge of understanding.

"Get some sleep, Mallory. I will be back soon. Try not to wake you. Tomorrow, they start the test run."

She sighed, ended the call, then turned back to the window. The rain's rhythm quickened, faster and heavier, like percussion warming up for an overture. Lightning flashed across the clouds, followed by a low, orchestral rumble.

She thought of the old operas her father loved, such as Tristan and Isolde and Twilight of the Gods, stories where sound and destiny were inextricably linked. She'd never cared much for them before, but now she understood: Wagner wasn't writing about love or power. He was writing about the notes that linger after the music ends.

Mallory pressed her palm to the glass. The thunder answered a half-second later, deep and resonant, as if the planet were clearing its throat.

Somewhere high above, on the other side of that storm, *The Gift* drifted in orbit around a sun 70 odd light-years away, listening, calibrating, and waiting for a signal it could trust. Down here, in a rain-soaked city, in a strange room filled with silence and loss, Mallory wondered whether the universe was about to start singing again.

On the far side of the planet, the storm Mallory watched had already circled the equator twice. To humans, it was a minor meteorological curiosity, but to the Sylvians monitoring reverberation fields, it was data gold. The rain distorted everything, from frequency and gravity readings to neural telemetry, as if an orchestra were retuning between movements.

At the cradle complex on Sylvee, Elijon stood beneath a canopy of translucent shielding that shimmered with every lightning strike. He could smell ozone and wet crystal; Sylvian rain always carried the scent of metal and memory.

Next to him, Nyla adjusted the calibration array, its six sounding towers bending in the wind like the ribs of a massive instrument.

"The atmosphere's absorbing half of our output," she muttered.

"Let it," Elijon said. "Maybe the planet's trying to sing along."

A crackle of static swept across the comm bands, soft at first, then pulsing. It wasn't random noise. Each burst arrived at a regular interval, a syncopation between thunderclaps. When projected onto the monitor, the pattern took on an eerie, deliberate cast.

"That's not weather," Nyla whispered.

"No," he said. "That's interference."

They exchanged a look that meant the same thing in any language: *someone else is playing this instrument.*

The Gift caught the same interference half a second later. Eleanor's analytics team logged the anomaly as an "unidentified high-gain harmonic intrusion," but she heard it differently. It was a chord she didn't recognize, a new theme entering the score.

She opened the main channel to *Sylvee.*

"Elijon, Nyla, are you hearing this?"

"Loud and clear," Elijon replied. "It's modulating."

"From where?"

"Not from us. It's coming *through* us."

The static grew, folding over itself in rising arpeggios. To an engineer, it looked like a malfunction; to a musician, it sounded intentional. Eleanor increased her gain. Beneath the distortion, she detected a faint carrier tone, human-sounding.

The Human Flaw Emerges

Thousands of kilometers away from where Mallory and Julian held each other, an array of military satellites positioned over the Pacific fired a coordinated burst of counter-signal intended to "stabilize" communications.

Hours earlier, a nervous coalition of governments had issued the order, fearful of losing control of the first-contact channel. No one had intended sabotage. The system had simply been designed to assert ownership, and it did so flawlessly.

Every dish on *The Gift's* menu was lit with a warning light.

Every harmonic on *Sylvee* was flattened into monotone.

The music died.

"They jammed us," Eleanor said quietly.

"Why?" Nyla's voice carried the disbelief of someone raised in a culture that had forgotten conflict.

"Because they could," Elijon answered. "Because they don't know what silence is."

The storm answered with another crash of thunder, drowning out the argument. Then something unexpected happened: the rainfall itself began pulsing in rhythm with the interference.

The drops struck the cradle's shielding in percussive unison, *tap-tap-rest-tap-tap-rest*, as if the planet had absorbed the static and were trying to resolve it.

"Listen," Nyla said.

"It's syncing," Elijon murmured. "The rain's compensating for the signal loss."

He realized then that nature was offering them a workaround. If they could capture the storm's harmonic pattern and feed it into the relay, they might transform the jamming into something usable, turning dissonance into a bridge.

The Counterpoint Solution

Hours passed in fevered collaboration. Nyla mapped rainfall frequency to response-field oscillations, while Elijon wrote an adaptive algorithm to fold the interference back onto itself.

Eleanor fed orbital telemetry into the mix, conducting a symphony of code.

The result was chaotic beauty: three civilizations, Sylvian, human, and planetary, tuning into one another through accident and intent. Each iteration brought the noise closer to coherence until, finally, the cradle emitted a single, unwavering note.

It was low at first, then spread outward, rippling through the storm. Clouds parted; light refracted. The static vanished, replaced by a harmonic so pure it vibrated in the soul.

"That's it," Eleanor whispered. "That's the pitch."

"What do we call it?" Nyla asked.

"Rain," Elijon said. "Just… rain."

They laughed, exhausted, the kind of laugh that follows surviving dissonance. Above and beyond them, *The Gift* recorded the signal and transmitted it back toward Earth, a message hidden in precipitation, impossible to weaponize or claim.

Closing Image

By dawn, the storm had passed. Pools of silver water gathered between the towers, reflecting the sun. In one, Nyla saw her own face ripple and said quietly:

"Maybe Origin isn't hiding, Elijon. Maybe it's learning to listen differently."

He looked toward the sky, where the last thunder rolled like applause.

"Then let's give them a new act."

Chapter Thirty-Two

"Rain"

\<Eleanor's Log: (+180 cycles post-contact)\>

December 2034

On Earth, it is the season of remembrance. Candles, lists, and songs sung once a year remind people that darkness has its own rhythm. The Sylvians do not name months, but tonight they will understand what December means.

The storm has cleared. The repaired signal rides its own echo, looping between planets like a refrain that refuses to fade. What began as interference has become an invitation.

Below, outside Julian's Seattle home, soon to be theirs, Mallory and he stand on a rain-darkened street, where distant windows glow with reflections of the global broadcast. The relay stations have patched into the Sylvian net; every speaker and earpiece hums with the recovered tone. The world stops, not from fear but from curiosity.

"They're singing," Mallory whispers.

From *The Gift's* orbiting array, Eleanor overlays the frequencies. Sylvian harmonic, Earth carrier wave, storm amplitude. She hears them fuse into a single choral body.

Within the blend, an Earth orchestra adds strings. A human conductor, caught up in wonder, quotes Bernstein's Hallelujah. The lyric is lost in translation, but the emotion endures: praise as physics.

The Sylvians respond instinctively. Their amplification halls open, and their instruments tune to the foreign key. The two choirs, one of flesh, one of light, find the same interval.

"This is not a transmission," Elijon murmurs inside Sylvee's dome.

"Then what is it?" Nyla asks.

"Reverberation," he answers. "The moment before understanding."

Eleanor closes her eyes. For a breath, she senses something beyond both species, an awareness that hums back through the carrier wave, a connection not as data but as recognition.

Sometimes, chaos hums in key. Sometimes, that's all the miracle we get.

An interference satellite, once a weapon of control, drifts into the harmonic field and begins to resonate. Panels glow, and circuits melt into light. It no longer jams; it amplifies. The machine joins the choir.

From space, the combined signal appears as a lattice of auroras winding around both worlds, a luminous thread binding curiosity and compassion.

Chapter Thirty-Three

"Roll Over Beethoven"

The skies of *Sylvee* bent differently at this time of year.

Light arrived, tired from its long flight around *The Torch*, refracting into ribbons of color that tangled across the horizon. In the Observatory of Innus, Rhen, First of Nine, leaned over the array and adjusted the harmonic filters until only one tone remained, a steady, pulse-soft whisper.

It had been three weeks since the Celebration of Versitra's Life. The morphic fields should have returned to equilibrium by then, yet something persisted, a single frequency that refused to fade. It shimmered just below perception, too orderly to be noise and too mournful to be mechanical.

Lessa Verrin, Second of Ten, entered without ceremony, her soft gray fur damp from the evening's rain.

"Still at it?" she asked.

Rhen glanced up, the console's faint glow painting his features.

"It's not in the database. Every pattern is cross-checked. It is a personal request."

"Personal?"

He gestured toward the screen. "No Sylvian frequency ever drifts alone. Yet this one bears her signature. It's Versitra's Passenger."

Lessa's breath caught. "Impossible."

"I thought so, too." He turned a control knob, magnifying the waveform. It trembled like a heartbeat.

"When she died, the Passenger should have dissolved into the planetary chorus, but it didn't. It clung to her fading harmony until both collapsed. Now it wanders, seeking another harmony strong enough to answer it."

The two stood in reverent silence. Outside, rain gathered on the observatory's glass, refracting the interior lights into a thousand tiny rainbows.

Lessa spoke first. "If this is true, it changes everything. *Passengers* are proof of balance; when one of us returns, the other returns with us. No one is ever alone."

Rhen nodded. "And yet, something still sings her name."

They listened. Through the array's speakers came a faint, irregular pulse of three notes: curiosity, integrity, and harmony, the Sylvian triad. But the third note faltered, incomplete.

Rhen whispered, "She's missing a chord."

Integrity

In the Hall of Harmonics, the Council of Thirteen convened beneath the great mirrors of refraction. Diosophene Hwager, First of Thirteen, presided with the stillness of polished stone. The echoes of Versitra's *Passenger* had unsettled the network; even those unaware of its origin felt a tremor in their meditations.

Rhen and Lessa stood before the Council. Behind them, light streamed through prisms set high in the walls, spilling across the floor in concentric patterns of violet and gold.

Diosophene's voice carried like measured music.

"Are your findings verified?"

Rhen inclined his head. "Yes, Diosophene. The anomaly is neither a glitch nor an echo. It is her Passenger, still active."

A murmur rippled through the chamber. One of the elders, a mathematician named Corri, Eighth of Twelve, leaned forward.

"The public must not know. It would undermine our understanding. A *Passenger* without a *Host* is… *coarseness.*"

Lessa's tone was quiet yet firm. "And yet it exists. Integrity is what binds our harmonies, not denial."

Diosophene regarded her for a long moment. "Integrity," she repeated. "They had it, especially Versitra. Even in their arguments, the cradle team held it close. True engineers."

Corri pressed on. "To tell this truth will sow dissonance. We are built to stay in tune."

Diosophene rose. "Lies do not resonate. Curiosity is distracted by the discourse; harmony is resentful, and the melody refuses to play along with a composition that lacks timbre. If we conceal this, we invite rot."

The Hall fell into a resonant hush. At last, she said, "Publish your findings. All of *Sylvee* will know what we know. If our harmony cannot withstand the truth, then it is not harmony at all."

Rhen bowed deeply. "Yes, First."

Lessa's eyes glistened. "Thank you."

As they departed, Diosophene turned to the mirrored ceiling, watching the rainlight ripple across it. "We are tested," she whispered. "May we not falter."

Harmony

The storm that night came without warning. Sudden. A tempest that lit both horizons at once. Elijon stood beneath the cradle's arch, the towers crackling with ionized mist. Nyla approached, her two hearts beating out of sync.

"You heard the Council's message," she said.

"I did."

"Do you think they were right?"

He hesitated. "Rightness is an interval, not a pitch. But perhaps we're closer to the true key."

Nyla looked toward the sky, where the auroras shifted in long, slow arcs. "I can feel it, the *Passenger's* pulse. It's been following me for days, as if waiting."

Elijon adjusted a console. "Perhaps it's searching for a bridge."

And then, through the static, a new sound emerged. It was faint, filtered through countless layers of atmospheric diffraction, yet unmistakable: a human voice, recorded decades earlier, its clarity intact.

"Thank you for listening to Side A."

The words rippled through the cradle's carrier field. Instruments shuddered as harmonics bent around the tone. Nyla clutched her chest, her eyes wide.

"She's calling."

And then, beneath that voice, another sound began… lower, slower, a pure vibration. The Passenger answering. Not in language, but in empathy made audible. Frequencies intertwined and overlapped until their interference vanished.

The storm's lightning changed color, no longer white but soft amber, the hue of sunrise through crystal. From the observatory, Rhen and Lessa watched their readings spike. The anomaly's waveform had merged with the external transmission.

"Two voices, one chord," Rhen murmured.

Across *Sylvee*, the harmonic network vibrated in unison. The citizens felt it as warmth, a fullness in the chest like the first breath after grief.

On Earth, observers at Mt. Stevens relayed recordings of auroral patterns forming deliberate shapes: spirals, filaments, and, finally, three faintly glowing concentric rings above the Pacific: Curiosity, integrity, and harmony.

Back at the cradle, the storm subsided. Nyla and Elijon stood in silence as the last waves of energy faded into the still air.

"Do you feel that?" she asked.

"I do."

"It's gone."

"No," Elijon said, a faint smile breaking through. "It's home."

Coda

Rhen, the First of Nine, wrote the report that would be entered into the archives that night. He titled it *Rigby's Chord*. The first line read:

"In the final days of the Season of Reflection, two worlds held their breath."

He hesitated before typing the following sentence, feeling the weight of the moment. "We are still listening," he wrote, then sealed the entry.

Outside, *Sylvee's* sun began its slow rise. In the quiet between the light, the morphic fields glowed like snowfields, softly humming with echoes from the day before.

Far away, aboard *The Gift*, Eleanor's sensors detected a faint harmonic drift; the signal she had sent was now returning, slightly delayed yet still intact.

She opened a new log.

"The bridge holds," she said. "End of transmission."

On the final page of the recording, her voice lingered in silence for three full seconds, long enough for the universe to answer.

Thank you for listening to Side A.

End of Book One - Rigby

Author's End Note

Rigby began with a nightlight that wasn't meant to be a nightlight.

There's a flatscreen on the wall across from my bed. On the bottom edge, a tiny LED stays lit, never turning off. In the middle of the night, during water runs, pet checks, and the usual negotiations with sleep, I'd see it: a quiet ember on a black sea. I started calling it a starship.

The name stuck, and with it came a practice. To get back to sleep, I'd tell myself a brief story about where the ship was headed tonight and who it might carry. Nothing elaborate. Two or three images. A line of dialogue. Seeds to plant. Enough narrative to lean on until morning.

For over a year now, those snippets have become tiny stories that have taught me my rhythms. They began to ask questions in return. What if a ship isn't something you board but something you notice? What if "signal" is just attention that refuses to blink? What if the smallest steady light can teach you how to navigate your work, your fears, and your friendships?

The book you're holding retains that original scale. *Rigby* isn't about spectacle first; it's about the quiet choices that become trajectories.

The LED on my wall didn't change brightness. I changed what I was willing to call it. That rename let me travel within the same four walls. It's a trick we get to play on ourselves: rename the ordinary, and it opens.

Chapter one hints at that origin: a small, unassuming light that keeps appearing until someone finally admits it's a guide. From there, the book delves into what I love most about music, science, and friendship: none works alone, and all improve when the truth is shared kindly.

If this story leaves you with one image, I hope it's simple: a dark room, a modest glow, and the sense that you can steer by it. We don't always need brighter stars.

Sometimes we just need to keep looking at those who shine steadily.

Thanks for reading and for traveling with us.

D. Dwayne Edwards

The following is a glimpse of

Biological Imparative

Book Two of A Conversation of Worlds

Chapter One - The Tuning

This was his third day on the trail called Rememberance. This journey is a longstanding rite of passage for Sylvians as they reach their two-hundredth year of life. Although the trek ends in the same place, the small village of Craymerche, nestled alongside a cove of a sea called Merche, there were many branches from which to choose. And those choices were always a collaboration between Host and Passenger.

Elijon, Third of Seven, stepped out from under the shade of trees onto a bright stretch of the trail lit by *The Torch*, their planet's sun. He was now nearly 950 meters up the side of the first of several mountains that formed the spine of this ancient trail. A trail that stretched nearly 750 kilometers. Three kilometers ahead, he faced a decision. His passenger was already singing a melody of direction and future in his chest. The song was hard to focus on, as his own mind was preoccupied with remembering the eyes of Nyla, Fourth of Eleven.

He paused to look up at the sky, feeling the warmth of the bright, blue cerulean day on the cocoa-colored fur on his face and head. He had seen Nyla just four days ago and remembered their last embrace. He recalled how warm her hand felt as their fingers parted, signaling the tentative start of his journey. He remembered stumbling over a rock and nearly falling backward as he walked, trying not to lose sight of her bright, sparkling eyes. She burst out laughing when he caught himself and shouted at him to focus or risk not returning intact. He had turned around and began his march.

www.ingramcontent.com/pod-product-compliance
Lightning Source LLC
Chambersburg PA
CBHW071253170626
46809CB00001B/197